"Have You Ever Made Love On A Balcony?" Callie Asked.

Surprised by her question, Brock grinned in the darkness. "No. Why?"

"Just curious. I imagine you've had sex in more interesting places than I have."

Setting down his glass of wine, he turned her to face him. "Do you want to make love on the balcony?"

"Maybe," she said a little defensively. "What if I do?"

He felt his grin grow. "Then we'll make love on the balcony."

She bit her lip. "Or maybe I'd like to sometime."

Backing against the wall, he pulled her with him. "I'll make a note to check the security of the railing," he said.

Bold, then timid. She was going to kill him.

Ah, but what a way to go.

Dear Reader,

Welcome to another passion-filled month at Silhouette Desire. Summer may be waning to a close, but the heat between these pages is still guaranteed to singe your fingertips.

Things get hot and sweaty with Sheri WhiteFeather's *Steamy Savannah Nights,* the latest installment of our ever-popular continuity DYNASTIES: THE DANFORTHS. *USA TODAY* bestselling author Beverly Barton bursts back on the Silhouette Desire scene with *Laying His Claim,* another fabulous book in her series THE PROTECTORS. And Leanne Banks adds to the heat with *Between Duty and Desire,* the first book in MANTALK, an ongoing series with stories told exclusively from the hero's point of view. (Talk about finally finding out what he's *really* thinking!)

Also keeping things red-hot is Kristi Gold, whose *Persuading the Playboy King* launches her brand-new miniseries, THE ROYAL WAGER. You'll soon be melting when you read about Brenda Jackson's latest Westmoreland hero in *Stone Cold Surrender.* (Trust me, there is nothing cold about this man!) And be sure to *Awaken to Pleasure* with Nalini Singh's superspicy marriage-of-convenience story.

Enjoy all the passion inside!

Melissa Jeglinski

Melissa Jeglinski
Senior Editor
Silhouette Desire

Please address questions and book requests to:
Silhouette Reader Service
U.S.: 3010 Walden Ave., P.O. Box 1325, Buffalo, NY 14269
Canadian: P.O. Box 609, Fort Erie, Ont. L2A 5X3

LEANNE BANKS
BETWEEN DUTY AND DESIRE

Published by Silhouette Books
America's Publisher of Contemporary Romance

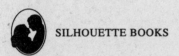

SILHOUETTE BOOKS

ISBN 0-373-76599-1

BETWEEN DUTY AND DESIRE

Visit Silhouette Books at www.eHarlequin.com

Printed in U.S.A.

LEANNE BANKS,

a *USA TODAY* bestselling author of romance and 2002 winner of the prestigious Booksellers' Best Award, lives in her native Virginia with her husband, son and daughter. Recognized for both her sensual and humorous writing with two Career Achievement Awards from *Romantic Times,* Leanne likes creating a story with a few grins, a generous kick of sensuality and characters that hang around after the book is finished. Leanne believes romance readers are the best readers in the world because they understand that love is the greatest miracle of all. Contact Leanne online at leannebbb@aol.com or write to her at P.O. Box 1442, Midlothian, VA 23113. An SASE for a reply would be greatly appreciated.

This book is dedicated to all of those
who have served in the United States Marine Corps.
I'm humbled by your discipline and dedication.

Prologue

"In war, you win or lose, live or die—and the difference is an eyelash."
—General Douglas MacArthur

The moon shone over the desert, reflecting on the land. As usual, Staff Sergeant Rob Newton was talking about his wife, Callie. Captain Brock Armstrong smiled inwardly at the story Rob told while the two of them conducted their routine patrol. Rob was clearly crazy about his wife. Brock's gaze shifted constantly around them and scanned the distance. He might be amused, but that didn't mean he wouldn't be careful.

Rob was laughing. An explosion split the air. Pain tore through Brock at the same time he heard Rob's scream. "Callie! Callie!"

His flesh burned and ached so much he couldn't

speak. Time crawled by in a haze of pain. Images blurred. He couldn't see out of his right eye. He tried to move, felt himself lifted, and heard the whir of a helicopter propeller. Help was on the way.

"Callie," he heard Rob mutter and managed to turn his head.

"Rob, you okay?"

"Don't let her crawl back in her hole and hide," *he said desperately. "Don't let her be a hermit. Don't let her—"*

"You need to calm down," another voice said. A medic? Brock wondered, feeling his sense of reality slip and slide. "You need to conserve your energy."

Everything went black.

Brock awakened, drenched in sweat. He opened his eyes, but the darkness closed around his throat like a vise. He reached for his bedside lamp and turned it on, then sat up in bed, breathing like he was running a marathon. Even though the wound was long healed, he instinctively rubbed his right eye. He hadn't been able to see out of the eye that night because blood from his head wound had pulled a curtain over his vision.

After months of physical therapy, he still limped. He might always limp. It didn't stop him from running. It wouldn't stop him from much, except being a Marine. He'd always known he wouldn't stay in the Corps forever, but he hadn't expected to receive a discharge with honors quite this soon.

He raked his hand through his hair. It was long and

needed a cut. Or not, he reminded himself. He wasn't required to keep it regulation length anymore.

He glanced around his room in the rehabilitation center and felt an edgy restlessness. He'd been here long enough. He was ready to move on, to leave this sense of shock and weakness behind. His body was growing stronger and his will was catching up.

He was sick of focusing on himself, sick of talking about himself during his sessions with the head-doctor.

Sighing, he slid to the edge of the bed and limped to the small window. He looked out into the night and remembered the last night he'd seen Rob Newton alive. The land mine had taken Rob and left Brock. Brock still didn't understand why, though he asked himself the question approximately every five minutes.

The staff shrink had told him he was suffering from survivor's guilt and it would take time.

Brock swallowed over a knot in his throat. "Thanks for nothing," he muttered.

Rob's cries for his wife echoed inside his brain. He closed his eyes against the clawing sensation inside him. Maybe he was never going to get over this. Maybe he was never going to feel at peace again. Sitting here in the rehab center wasn't going to solve anything. He could finish the rest of his therapy on his own.

He had to find a way to live with himself, a way to assuage his guilt. He snorted. *Mission Impossible.* What could he do for a dead man?

He thought again of Rob's widow. Maybe, just maybe, he could live with himself a little more easily if he honored Rob's last request.

One

Marine Lingo Translation
Alpha Unit: Marine's spouse.

He knew her favorite color was blue.

He knew she was allergic to strawberries, but sometimes ate them anyway.

He knew her hazel eyes changed colors depending on her mood.

He knew she had a scar at the top of her thigh from a bike wreck she'd had when she was a child.

Brock knew Callie Newton intimately, even though he'd never met her. That would change in approximately ninety seconds, he thought, as he lifted his hand to knock on the weathered wooden door to her South Carolina beach cottage. The salty scent of the ocean was a nice change from the antiseptic smell of the rehab center.

His leg aching from being wedged into the small seat in the commercial jet that had brought him here, he leaned against the outside wall of the house for a moment. When there was no answer, he shifted and knocked again, this time more loudly.

He heard the sound of scrambling feet and a muffled shriek, then more scrambling and the door finally flew open. A woman with mussed shoulder-length strawberry-blond hair shielded her eyes with her hands as if she were seeing the sun for the first time today. Dressed in a wrinkled oversize white T-shirt and faded denim shorts that emphasized long lithe pale legs, Callie Newton squinted her eyes at him. "Who are—"

"Brock Armstrong," he said, wondering if she had any idea that the white T-shirt she wore revealed her nipples. He lifted his gaze from her chest. "I knew—"

"Rob," she finished for him, her voice softening. Her eyes darkened with sadness. "He talked about you in the e-mails and letters he sent me. The Dark Angel."

Brock felt an odd twist at hearing his nickname again. His buddies had given it to him because his hair and eyes were dark, along with his mood. Hell, before the accident, he'd been angry for as long as he could remember. He had been locked in combat with his stepfather since puberty. The "angel" part of the name was given because he'd pulled several guys out of tough spots.

Not Rob, though, he thought, feeling another hard

tug in his gut. He hadn't been able to pull Rob out of his tough spot.

Callie chewed the inside of her bottom lip and waved her hand toward the house. "Come in."

Brock followed her into the dark interior of the cottage. He heard her whack her leg against an end table and she made a quick hissing sound of pain.

"You want me to turn on a light or open one of the blinds?" he asked.

"No. I'll do it," she muttered, moving toward a large window and adjusting the blinds so that the sun illuminated the room. The couch was covered with a dark throw, the walls were bare of pictures and the hardwood floor was rugless. "I worked late last night—well, really into the morning," she added. "I guess I overslept." She whipped around to face him, stumbling again.

Brock instinctively grabbed her arms to keep her upright. With one red-gold strand over one eye, she looked at him and he was close enough to count her eyelashes and freckles. He'd heard stories about the placement of some of those freckles.

"What time is it anyway?" she asked in a sleep-husky voice that reminded him of sex.

Hell, everything reminded him of sex. It had been too damn long since he'd gotten any. "Fourteen hun—" He stopped, remembering he didn't need to speak in military time. "Two o'clock in the afternoon."

She winced. "I didn't realize it was so late." A cat prowled into the room and wrapped around her ankles. "Bet you're hungry, Oscar," she said to the feline then glanced at him. "I'll start some coffee."

She took a step, nearly tripped over the cat, righted herself then left the room.

A little klutzy in the morning, he recalled Rob telling him and felt a twitch of humor. Only this wasn't morning, at least not for most people.

Brock glanced around the spare, bare room. It didn't feel right. Rob had described Callie as if she never took a break from creating and decorating. Every room had a theme. She didn't know the meaning of the word bland. He frowned. This room was definitely bland.

He wandered down the hallway where he heard water running from a faucet. The kitchen was small, but sunny with a clean sink and clean counters. There was no kitchen table. Instead a chair stood at the end of the counter where he spotted a sketch pad, a box of Frosted Lucky Charms and Little Debbie Swiss Cake Rolls.

Uh-oh. Swiss Cake Rolls were PMS and deadline food. Brock approached her warily. "Are you on deadline?"

She nodded. "I got behind when Rob—" She broke off and sighed. "I couldn't draw for a while. I can now, but I'm not sure any of it is right. I'm still not reaching for happy, light colors and I'm supposed to be illustrating happy, light books. Three of them. I've done all the rainy, sad, gray scenes," she said, staring expectantly at the coffeemaker. "Four times."

A suspicion was forming in his gut. "Looks like

a nice little island," he ventured. "Do you like your neighbors?"

She ran her hand through her hair. "I haven't had time to meet them. I don't get out much."

His suspicion intensified. "I'm staying here for a while. Can you recommend a couple of restaurants?"

She bit her lip. "Y'know, I haven't had a lot of time. I've done most of my grocery shopping at the quick-mart."

He nodded, rubbing his chin. So Rob's concern for Callie had been justified—she'd turned into a hermit.

The coffee flowed into the carafe and she pulled two mugs out of the cabinet. Pouring the coffee, she looked up. "I don't have cream. Would you like sugar?"

He shook his head and accepted the mug she offered. "Black is fine."

She cradled her mug in both hands and took a quick sip then glanced up at him. "Rob really admired you."

"It was mutual. Rob was well-liked and respected. He was a mechanical whiz and he talked about you all the time."

She rolled her eyes. "He must have bored you guys to death."

He shook his head. "He gave us a nice break from the tension." He paused. "I'm sorry I couldn't make it to his funeral. The doctor wouldn't let me out of the hospital."

"Understandable," she said, lowering her gaze to

her cup so that her eyelashes shielded her expression from him. "You were hurt when the mine…" She shrugged as if she didn't want to finish. "I didn't want Rob to join the Marines. It was one of the few things we argued about."

"Why? Too dangerous?"

"At the time he joined, I don't think I realized how dangerous it could be. I just didn't want to move and move and move. I wanted us to make a home, a haven, and stay there forever."

"But you moved here after he died," Brock pointed out.

She shook her head. "Too many memories. I felt like I was bumping into him, into our dreams, every three minutes." She met his gaze. "So why are you here?"

Not ready to reveal Rob's last request, he glanced down at his leg. "I'm almost finished with my rehabilitation and I couldn't stand being tied to the center one more minute. I decided a few weeks at the beach before I take my job sounded good."

"Why this beach?" she asked, her eyes skeptical. She was waking up and she wasn't stupid.

"It's quiet, not too commercial." He cracked a grin. "If I fall on my face when I take my morning run, no one will see me and laugh."

Her gaze shifted. She was still skeptical, but more amused. "Something tells me you don't have much experience falling on your face."

"Not until this year."

Her half smile faded. "I'm sorry."

"I'm sorry about Rob."

"Thanks. Me, too," she said and gave him a considering glance. "If this was a duty call, consider
it done."

He nodded, but inside he was shaking his head. The
woman lived at the beach, but her skin was as white
as the sand and the circles under her eyes were vio-
let. She looked too thin and as though she were stuck
in neutral. He needed to at least get her into first gear.

Brock settled into his condo which was about a
quarter-mile north of Callie's. Sitting on the balcony,
he watched the waves rhythmically rolling in and
felt a measure of peace wash through him. The ocean
wasn't about war. It changed every second, but in
many ways remained constant. Watching the tide
provided the best therapy he'd been given in months,
and Lord knew the military had made damn sure
he'd received a truckload of therapy.

As he climbed into bed and fell asleep, an image
of Callie Newton drifted through his mind. He wondered what she was doing right this minute. Was she
staring at a blank canvas? Was she drawing yet another dark picture? Or was she falling asleep just
like he was? He remembered being fascinated by the
photograph of her that Rob had proudly displayed.
She'd been laughing with abandon. She'd looked
like the female equivalent of sunshine. She and Rob
could have posed for matching bookends of the all-

American boy and girl. Rob had miraculously managed to get through boot camp without having his upbeat attitude beat out of him. Rob had been a nice uncynical guy, not like Brock. Brock had enough cynicism for a dozen men. Maybe that was why he'd been drawn to Rob and his stories about his wife. They'd seemed fresh and innocent. Brock couldn't remember feeling fresh and innocent, not since his father died when he was seven years old.

His mind drifted back to Callie. Even though the sadness in her eyes twisted his gut, something about being in her presence made him breathe a little easier. He sensed she might demand perfection of herself and in her work, but she didn't demand it of others. He frowned, wondering why she seemed sexy to him.

Her hair was a seductive red-gold curtain and her white skin emphasized her femininity. Her lips reminded him of a juicy plum and that damn T-shirt had made him want to play hide-and-seek with her curves.

He felt himself grow hard and swore under his breath. His attraction to Callie wasn't personal. He was frustrated—sexually, personally, mentally. Tossing off the covers, he walked naked to the shower. *Forget the cold water.* He turned on the warm spray and stepped inside where he could take care of at least part of his frustration with any woman he chose to picture in his mind.

* * *

The following morning, he rose at six o'clock. The Marine Corps had conditioned him to rise early. He didn't know if he'd ever be able to sleep in again. He fixed a breakfast of scrambled eggs, toast and coffee and read the newspaper, showered and dressed in running shorts and a tank, then walked down the beach to Callie's cottage at ten o'clock.

The first step to feeling normal was sleeping at night and working during the day. Callie was like a baby who had her nights and days mixed up. She needed a little help to deconfuse them. He rapped on the front door to the darkened, quiet house and waited. And waited. He rubbed the toe of his running shoe on a rough place in the concrete on her porch then knocked again.

He heard a loud bang and "Ouch!" and shook his head. The door jerked open and she squinted up at him. "Why do I feel like I've done this before?"

"Sorry. I thought you'd be awake by now," he fudged. "I remember hearing that you liked to run, so I wondered if you would like to join me this morning for a slow jog. My leg's not a hundred percent, so I have to move a little more slowly than I'd like."

"Run?" she echoed and looked outside. "Now? What time is it?"

"Ten o'clock," he said.

"Oh," she murmured, pushing her hair from her face. "I had a late night last night working on a drawing," she said. "That I probably won't use," she added in a dark, disgusted tone, and sighed.

"If you're not up to it…" he ventured, checking to see if she had enough fire in her to rise to the challenge.

She frowned. "I'm up to it," she retorted waspishly. "I may be a little rusty because it's been a while, but I'm up to it."

He nodded, approving the hint of a kick in her response. That was a good sign. "You want me to wait out here while you change?"

She glanced down at her nightshirt as if she'd just realized she still had it on. Her cheeks colored. "Yeah, I should have— I was—" She shrugged and waved him inside. "You can come in. It won't take me long."

"Thanks," he murmured and followed her in the door, catching a draft of her sweet, sleepy scent. It was a fresh, sexy smell that made him want to bury his face in her hair. The thought took him by surprise and he shook his head.

She hurried down the hallway and the cat greeted him with a sniff then dismissed him. He'd never understood the appeal of cats. Felines didn't come when they were called. They expected to be fed and sheltered, yet pretty much disdained their owners. Now, dogs were a different story.

Callie returned with her hair pulled back in a ponytail. She wore a tight sporty tank top and a little pair of shorts that rode below her belly button. A few of the nurses at the rehab center had come on to him, but none of them had been dressed like this.

Damn, he'd been locked up entirely too long. He was beginning to feel like a raging bundle of hormones. Before the accident, he'd had his share of women. He'd never had any problem finding a willing woman. Rob had said he went through women with the same ease a lot of men went through a six-pack of beer. It wasn't far from the truth. He'd always made it clear he wasn't making any promises—he didn't want to put in the time a *relationship* required.

Ungluing his gaze from Callie's bare belly, he raked his hand through his hair. "You ready?"

She moved her head in an indecisive circle. "Let's go."

They hit the beach and twenty-three minutes later Brock was afraid she was going to keel over before she'd tell him she'd had enough. "There's a coffee shop. You want to stop?"

She came to an abrupt stop and met his gaze with a mixture of wariness and relief. "Do you?"

She was clearly prickly, so he took a light approach. "If you get heat exhaustion, it would be a real hassle to have to haul you back to your cottage with my bum leg."

She frowned. "Are you denigrating my level of physical fitness?"

"Not at all. You look physically *fine* to me. You just might be a little out of practice."

She opened her mouth as if to protest then seemed to think better of it.

"Let me buy you breakfast," he said, moving toward the coffee shop.

She groaned. "I'm so overheated I'll never be able to eat," she muttered.

"We'll see," he said.

Twenty-five minutes later—after Callie had downed three glasses of ice water, a glass of orange juice and a cup of coffee—she was tearing into her hotcakes, eggs and bacon as if she hadn't eaten in days.

"More syrup?" he asked, lifting the small pitcher.

She shook her head. "Thanks, no."

"More pancakes?" he asked, unable to keep his humor from his voice.

She glanced up at him with her mouth full of pancake and searched his gaze. She chewed and swallowed. "Go ahead and say it," she said, taking a sip of coffee.

"Say what?"

"That you told me I'd want breakfast. How did you know, anyway?"

"If what I saw on your kitchen counter was any indication of what was inside the cabinets then you must be craving some substance. Cereal can't satisfy forever. How long has it been since you've had some protein?"

"Not that long," she said with a trace of defensiveness in her voice.

He nodded. "Good. What'd you have?"

Chewing another bite of pancake, she blinked then looked away. "Last week I had some cheese…"

Her words had faded and turned unintelligible. "Excuse me? You had some cheese what?"

She frowned at him and played with the strawberry garnish on her plate. "I had some cheese crackers last week."

"Oh," he said, swallowing a grin. "Good to know you're sticking with the pyramid diet plan."

She picked up the strawberry then set it down. "I don't put a high priority on eating when I'm on deadline."

"Hey, I'm with you. When I've been in a crunch, I've eaten peanut M&M's and coffee."

"Well it's good to know you bow to your baser urges every now and then. I suspect it doesn't happen very often."

Not as often as he'd like to give in to his baser urges, he thought as he watched her lift the strawberry to her lips.

"Are you sure you want to itch all day?"

Her eyes widened and she set the strawberry down. "How did you know I was allergic to them?"

"Rob told me."

She rolled her eyes in disgust. "What a big mouth. What else did he tell you?"

"Just your complete family, health, educational, professional and romantic history."

"Well that stinks," she said. "You know everything about me and I don't know diddly about you except how smart he said you were and what a good leader he said you were and how fast he said you could run."

Brock felt an itchy discomfort at the thought of Rob's praise. "Can't run all that fast anymore."

"You can outrun me."

"Yeah, but you're totally out of sh—" He broke off as her eyes widened.

"I didn't have any Marine training to get your buff body," she said, lifting her chin. "Look at those muscles," she said, pointing to his arms. "You're just a show-off."

Brock chuckled at the same time he felt a strange rush of pleasure at her backhanded compliment. He gave her feminine curves a once-over then a twice-over for good measure. "Trust me. Your body is no hardship on the eyes."

She met his gaze and something snapped and flickered between them.

She cleared her throat and took a sip of ice water. "You're too kind," she murmured. "Thanks for breakfast. I think I can walk back to my cottage now." She smiled. "See, now I have the excuse that I shouldn't exercise after I've just eaten."

"True," he said, tossing a few bucks on the table to cover the tip. "Must have felt great, though, your blood pumping through your veins, the ocean breeze on your face, the sun shining down," he teased.

"The onset of heatstroke," she added, deadpan. "Are you sure the Marines don't train you to have a sadistic streak a mile wide?" she asked over her shoulder as they left the coffee shop.

"Nah," he said, his gaze latching onto her curvy backside. *You can look, but you can't touch.* "Masochists. We're all masochists."

Two

Marine Lingo Translation
Semper Gumby: Unofficial motto—
Always Flexible.

The next morning when Brock knocked on Callie's door, she was still in her nightshirt, but she was awake. *Progress,* he thought as she opened the door. "I'm running a little late. I got on a roll and didn't go to bed until the middle of the night," she said. "Although I'd planned to go to bed early so I wouldn't embarrass myself during our run this morning. Looks hot out there."

"Eighty-two and the humidity is—"

"Three hundred percent," she said with a wry grin. "One of the charms of living at the shore. It won't take me but a minute to change. Are you sure you don't want to go by yourself? I'll just hold you back."

No, she wouldn't. He'd already gone for a run

once this morning. "Not a chance. Hey, when are you going to show me your etchings?"

"I don't know," she said warily. "I haven't been feeling all that confident about my work lately. I think I'd rather show my scars than my art."

"Is that your appendectomy scar or your bicycle accident scar?" he asked.

Her eyes widened like saucers. "There you go again. Geez, was there anything he did *not* tell you?"

"I'll tell you when I notice something."

She gave a grumble of disgust. "Well, this has got to change. It's not fair. You're going to have to cough up some information about yourself."

He shrugged. "No problem. There's not much to tell though. I'm not nearly as fascinating as you are."

She rolled her eyes. "Yeah, right." She wagged her finger at him. "Give me a minute and be prepared to answer some questions while we're running."

A few minutes later, they hit the beach and she immediately started shooting questions at him. "Favorite color?"

"Same as yours, blue," he said.

She smiled and shook her head. "Birthplace?"

"Columbus, Ohio. You were born in Pine Creek, North Carolina."

"What will you do now that you're out of the Marines?"

"Architecture. I majored in architecture in college and specialized in structural analysis. I'll be working for a major firm in Atlanta."

She wrinkled her nose. "I don't like big cities."

"Yeah, I know. Rob mentioned that. Atlanta's got a lot going on. That was my best job offer and it seemed like a good place to start over."

She slowed. "Do you mind when people mention your military career?"

"No," he said, shaking his head. "I just don't want to talk about it a lot. As you know, it didn't end the way I thought it would."

Her gaze softened with sadness and sympathy. "You've had a rough recovery, haven't you?"

He wanted to say that it could have been worse, but he didn't want to make her feel bad. "My drill instructor from boot camp visited me when I'd been in the hospital just a couple of weeks and told me if I started feeling sorry for myself, he was going to round up his men and hold a Victoria's Secret panty party for me."

"How charming. Was that supposed to be motivation?"

He chuckled. "In a way. Sergeant Roscoe is an expert at motivation. He called us all kinds of flattering, uplifting names in boot camp. Ladies, knuckleheads, maggots— I probably shouldn't repeat any more."

"What a jerk. Every time Rob told me about boot camp, it made me nuts. It's so barbaric, so disrespectful."

"The point was to learn respect and loyalty in a short amount of time."

"Well, I don't see why they had to be so rude about it."

"It offends your artistic sensibilities," he said, unable to keep a grin from his face.

"It offends my every sensibility," she huffed, shaking her head. "Okay, another question. Your favorite food? Let me guess, steak and potato."

He couldn't resist teasing her. "I was going to say quiche or those little cucumber sandwiches they serve at tea."

She did a double take. "Oh, you're pulling my leg."

"You have two very nice legs. Why can't I pull one?"

Her lips lifted in a smile and she chuckled. "You're funnier than I would have predicted," she said.

He looked at her eyes. Still not sparkling the way they had in that photograph he'd looked at so many times when he'd been in the desert. *You're sadder than I expected,* he thought, but didn't say it aloud. He wanted to change it. It was strange as hell, but he wanted to see her laughing with abandon again. He wondered what it would take.

"You're trying to distract me into slowing down, so you don't get a good run," he said, picking up the pace just a little.

She made a face. "Haven't we already had a *good* run?"

Brock just gave an evil chuckle.

By the time they returned to her cottage, she had extracted from him bits of his family history and even some of his romantic history. His leg was starting to ache.

She must have noticed his limp. "Come in and have something to drink before you leave."

"Do you have anything?" he teased, reminding her of her bare cupboards.

She gave a moue of reproach. "Of course I do. I have water and coffee. I may even have a flat soda."

"How can I resist? Throw in a tour of your studio and it's a deal."

She wrinkled her nose as she pulled open her screen door. "Do I have to?"

"You could always show me your scars," he suggested.

Her gaze met his and he felt the crackling sensation zip between them again. "Okay, I'll show you my studio, but make it snappy."

Curious, he accepted a glass of water and followed her into a back room with only bedsheets for window coverings. It was filled with drawings, and the floor was carpeted with discarded, balled-up sheets of paper. A large table sat before the window.

He drew closer to a casually arranged collection of drawings of a little girl with wide eyes and blond hair that stuck out. In one, the clouds hovering over her had wispy faces that looked like monsters. In another, the wind whipped her against a tree. In another, rain drenched her even though she carried a red umbrella.

"She doesn't look like she has a lot of luck with weather," he said.

"Those are the dark pictures I told you about. Now I need to do the bright, happy, sunny pictures. I'm not sure how."

"You could fake it," he suggested.

"Fake it?" she echoed in disapproval.

"You could pretend to be in a bright, happy, sunny mood for a few hours and see what happens. We had to pretend to like a lot of things we really didn't like when I was on active duty."

She looked skeptical. "I don't know. Art is about being authentic."

He nodded and shrugged. "Just a suggestion." He glanced around the room and his gaze fell on a picture of the ocean on a cloudy day. The way she'd mingled blue, gray and white drew him. A discarded red life preserver drifted aimlessly.

"What do you think of it?" she asked.

"Do you want me to be honest?"

"Yeah, I can take it," she said with a smile in her voice.

"There's something moody and sexy about it. The red of the life preserver reminds me of red lipstick. This isn't going in your kid book, is it?"

"No." She laughed. "I guess you could say this is one of my few grown-up pictures."

"Ever thought about having a show?" he asked.

"Not unless I'm forced."

"Why not?"

She shrugged. "I don't know. I think it might be easier to walk naked down Main Street. I put so much of myself in my paintings."

"Hmm," he said, looking again at her grown-up picture.

"What does 'hmm' mean?" she asked, looking at him curiously.

"I just had a philosophical thought," he said and grinned. "Don't worry. It'll pass."

"What?" she asked. "What's your philosophical thought?"

"What do you see as the purpose of your art?" he asked, thinking back to the art appreciation course he'd taken in college.

She paused thoughtfully. "I think my art may be multipurpose. There's self-expression, of course, and with Phoebe over there, there's sympathy and emotion. Identification. Haven't we all had a bad day when the weather was horrible?"

"So your pictures make people feel less alone," he said.

She paused again then slowly smiled. "I guess so."

"And a show might give some different people the opportunity to enjoy your drawings and feel less alone," he said.

"I hadn't thought of it that way. I just break out in a cold sweat thinking about exposing myself." She wrapped her arms around herself. "Rob always wanted me to do a show." She closed her eyes. "But Rob also wanted me to skydive, ride a bicycle with no hands and go skinny-dipping in high school."

"Extreme boyfriend," he said with a chuckle.

She smiled and met his gaze. "That would be

right. He was always dragging me off on one adventure or another."

"Did you like it?"

"Sometimes. Sometimes I just wanted to be my little boring self drawing on a pad of paper while I sat under the kitchen table."

"Now, see, I would think it could get a little cramped under the kitchen table."

"Think of it as a pup tent. It felt safe."

She was so freakin' cute he had the overwhelming urge to take her in his arms and make her feel safe. Which wasn't like Brock at all. Maybe that concussion had left permanent damage? "How'd the skinny-dip turn out?"

She tossed him a sideways glance. "We got caught. Well, I guess I should say I got caught. When we heard someone drive up, Rob pulled on his shorts, but my clothes had disappeared. I stayed in that creek so long my entire body turned blue."

Brock swallowed a chuckle. "That's a new one. I never heard that story."

"Probably because I told Rob I wouldn't speak to him again if he told anyone."

Brock saw her expression change from amused frustration to wistfulness and felt his gut twist. He shifted his stance and the papers rustled beneath his feet, distracting her.

"Look at this mess," she said. "I need to pick these up and toss them."

He bent down to help her. "I noticed there was more on the floor than on the walls or easels."

She laughed. "A lot more. One of the secrets of

getting past a block is not being afraid to waste some paint by drawing something that really stinks."

He started to uncurl one of the balled-up pieces of discarded paper and she immediately caught his hand.

"Oh, no. Absolutely not. I let you look at my studio, but I draw the line at allowing you to look at my stinkers."

"How do you know they're really stinkers? I might think they're good."

"It doesn't matter what you think. It matters what I think."

He glanced down at her slim, artistic fingers over his larger hand and felt an odd stirring inside him. He looked up into her resolute don't-mess-with-me gaze. "Are you sure you've never been a drill instructor? You sure can be bossy for a little thing."

"I may not be able to control what goes on outside this room, and I'm not always happy with what I create inside this room, but I make the rules for this room."

"The goddess of your little corner of the universe," he said, understanding her need for control.

"I wouldn't use the term 'goddess,'" she said dryly.

"You're not looking at you," he said and surrendered the ball of discarded paper even though he was curious as hell.

She stared at him and he felt the electrical zap between them again. She must have felt it, too, because he saw her catch her breath. She quickly pulled her hand from his.

"He told me you were good with the ladies," she said. "Flattering a woman must be second nature to you."

He shrugged, but didn't say anything. He knew a no-win conversation with a woman when he saw it coming.

"What? No answer? What are you thinking?"

"You don't really want to know."

"Yes, I do."

He shook his head and scooped up another piece of paper. "Nah."

He felt her hand on his arm. "I want to know. Fair is fair. You know all about me."

Uncomfortable, he sighed. "Okay, you're gonna think this is cocky as hell, but I don't have to flatter women. I haven't had to work that hard to get a woman's attention."

She opened her mouth then shut it. "That's pretty cocky."

"I told you."

"Right," she said. "Rob told me you didn't keep any of them around too long, either."

He shouldn't care what she might think of his lack of commitment, but he did. "I never made promises I couldn't keep. Everything always felt temporary—in college, in the Corps."

She nodded, but he could tell she didn't understand and it bothered him. "I don't know why I always had it easy with females."

"Oh, I know," she said. "They want to tame you. You have this dark, restless look about you that makes women want to domesticate you."

"You said women," he told her in a low voice. "Does that include you?"

"N-no, no no no," she said, taking a step back. "I may illustrate children's books, but I don't live in never-never land. I've never gone for the dark, brooding type. They always seemed like too much work and angst."

Glimpsing a reluctant fascination in her gaze that belied her words, he casually took a step toward her. "You think I'm dark and brooding?"

"Well, you're not exactly a laugh a minute," she said, biting her lip.

"Do I make you nervous, Callie?"

Her eyes said *yes,* but she shook her head. "Not really."

He shook his head and narrowed his eyes. "Why do I make you nervous?"

She crossed her arms over her chest. "I just said that you don't."

"I'm not convinced."

She looked away from him and sighed. "You're just different than what I'm used to."

"You're used to the boy-next-door dragging you off on little adventures."

"Yeah." She pushed a strand of hair behind her ear, and the expression in her eyes held warring glints of grief and a forbidden curiosity that was all too easy for him to understand, because he felt the same burning curiosity about Callie.

Three

Marine Lingo Translation
Commando: Not wearing underwear.

Brock didn't see Callie for more than ten minutes during the next three days. Shin splints prevented her from running on Tuesday and it rained nearly nonstop on Wednesday and Thursday as tropical depression Bettina revved up to tropical storm Bettina.

Brock ran despite the rain. He struggled with what he needed to do next to get through to Callie. He also struggled with how much he thought about her when she wasn't around. He put it down to unfinished business. As soon as he could help Callie out of the hole she was hiding in, she wouldn't occupy so much of his mind and he would be able to move on.

When the lights started flickering in the afternoon, he thought about her bare cupboard and nearly bare refrigerator and made a quick trip to the grocery store before everything shut down. By the time he knocked on her front door, he and the bags he carried were drenched.

Callie opened the door and stared at him. "What are you doing—" She broke off and tried to take one of the bags from his arms, but he held tight.

Her eyebrows puckering in a frown, she tugged on his arm. "Come in, you nutcase. Don't you know there's a hurricane coming?"

"That's why I brought you some food," he said, allowing her to guide him to the kitchen where he set the bags on the counter. "I figured by the time you realized you didn't have anything to eat the convenience store would be closed and you would be hungry and SOL."

"SOL?" she repeated with a confused expression on her face. "Oh, *surely out of luck,*" she translated.

"That's the Disney version," he muttered.

She shook her head. "I could get offended by your lack of confidence in my ability to take care of myself," she fumed as she began to unload the bags.

"I got bread, milk, eggs, cheese, pancake mix, a couple of steaks, a few frozen and canned staples and chocolate-covered peanuts."

Her eyes rounded and she dug through the second bag and pulled out the box. "Double dipper chocolate-covered peanuts! Oh, you have no idea how much I love—" She broke off and tossed him a sideways glance then rolled her eyes. "Oh, yes you do. Rob must have told you."

Brock nodded.

"Okay, in exchange for your gift of double dippers I can forgive your lack of faith in me."

His lips twitched at her cockeyed point of view. "That's mighty generous of you," he said, feeling a strange warmth from seeing her again even though she'd scolded him.

Her gaze fell over him and she gasped. She touched his damp cheek with her soft hand. "You're drenched and I've been standing here fussing at you. Do you want to shower? No, don't answer. You should shower before the electricity goes completely out—and it will," she said knowingly. "If you hurry, I can put your clothes in the dryer. So hurry," she said, shooing him into the hall. She grabbed a couple of towels from the closet and pushed them into his hands.

"Just toss your clothes out the door as soon as you get undressed."

"I can handle being wet. It's not a big deal," he said.

"It is when you don't have any dry clothes to change into."

"I've got plenty back at my cottage."

She blinked. "Oh, I thought you were going to join me for dinner."

Her husky invitation did something weird to his gut. "I guess I could."

Her lips curved in a slow smile. "Then if we want to eat, we'd better hurry before the electricity goes out."

His stomach growling at the thought of steak, he stepped into the bathroom, shucked his clothes and tossed them in the hall as she'd suggested. He turned her shower on hot, quickly lathered his body and rinsed. He had to concede Callie had been right. The shower felt great. It reminded him of how good a shower had felt coming in from the field. A shower followed by a couple of cold beers, a hot meal and a hotter woman provided a little respite from the uncertainty.

He rubbed himself dry with one towel and ran his fingers through his hair. Glancing around her bathroom, he saw her silk bathrobe hanging on the back of the door and gave in to the urge to touch it. He suspected her skin was just as soft, only warmer. He thought of her rosebud mouth and licked his own lips. Where were these thoughts coming from? Shaking his head to clear it, he wrapped the second towel around his waist and ventured into the hallway. He heard the rattle of pots and pans in the kitchen and turned in that direction.

"Need some help?" he asked as he rounded the corner.

Callie looked up from the bag of frozen mixed vegetables she was pouring into a pot and stared openmouthed at him. He could feel her hazel gaze track every inch of his bare skin from his throat and shoulders to his chest down to his abdomen over the towel that covered him to just above his knees.

Her hand shifted and the vegetables began to spill onto the stove top.

"Whoa," he said, stepping forward to reposition her hand.

Her hand trembled beneath his.

"Sorry, I didn't mean to startle you."

She jerked her hand away from his as if he'd scorched her. She shook her head and backed away, her gaze drifting to his chest repeatedly. "No, I just—uh—" She swallowed and met his gaze.

Brock glanced down at his bare torso and saw the tracks of his wounds from the explosion. He'd grown accustomed to the scars, but Callie hadn't ever seen them. His gut twisted. Maybe his scars made Callie think of Rob. "Is it the scars?"

She blinked and shook her head. "Uh, no," she said sounding surprised. "No, it's—"

"It's what?"

Embarrassment crossed her face and she looked away. "It's the muscles."

It took him a moment to comprehend what she'd said and when he did, he felt a roar of pleasure he couldn't recall feeling in a long time. So, her emotions weren't totally dead after all. That was good. It was part of the plan. Her attraction to him, however, wasn't part of the plan, but he wasn't inclined to discourage it at the moment.

"Thanks for the compliment," he said quietly, feeling a grin play around his lips.

She risked a glance at him. "I'm sure tons of women have complimented your body."

"Not lately," he said.

"Whose choice is that?"

He shrugged. "It hasn't been a priority." His body would disagree.

"Do you think you're not as attractive because of your scars?"

"I haven't really cared," he said, and it was true. "I feel different now. It's more than the limp and the scars. I haven't figured it all out yet."

"Inside," she said thoughtfully.

"Yeah." He inhaled and caught a whiff of beef broiling. "The steaks aren't burning, are they?"

"Oh no!" Her eyes widened and she jerked open the oven door. A sizzling sound immediately filled the air and she pulled the steaks from the oven. "They don't look too bad, but you're out of luck if you wanted yours rare."

"If it's not as tough as shoe leather, I'll consider it perfect," he said and glanced at the toaster oven. "You think the bread—"

"Yes, I do," she said, pulling out the biscuits. "Oh, look, the veggies are boiling. They won't take any time. I think you got some margarine," she said, pulling a stick from the refrigerator. "We're almost set."

Brock grabbed plates and cups from the cupboard, Callie collected the flatware and, within moments, they took their plates into the den to eat.

"Sorry I don't have a kitchen table," she said as she sat on the floor across from him. "That's on my to-do list."

The lights flickered and he could almost feel her hold her breath. They came back on and she sighed.

"I know they'll probably go out for hours, but I want it put off as long as possible."

"Are you afraid of the dark?" he asked, then took a bite of steak that was slightly overcooked, but still tasty.

"No," she said, taking a sip of water. "And yes.

"I'm not really afraid of the dark. I just don't like not being able to have light when I want it."

He nodded, amused. "So it's more of a convenience issue."

"For the most part," she said. "There's also the side effect of how other senses are sharpened to compensate for the one you can't use."

"Things that go bump in the night."

"Yeah, aliens under the bed, in the closet." She took a bite of steak and swallowed.

"But you're not really afraid."

"Right," she said, as she opened a biscuit and poured honey on it. "If I keep telling myself that, it will come true, right?"

Brock chuckled. "Yeah, right."

"Are you afraid of anything? Oh, wait, you're a Marine, so you're not allowed to be afraid."

"Everybody's afraid of something, Callie."

She met his gaze, and understanding and something more flickered between them.

"I just try not to let my fears get in my way, and when they do, I do something about them." He took another bite of steak and thought about why he was here with Callie right now. It was because he was afraid he would never be able to sleep at night and face his image in the mirror each morning if he didn't at least try to help Rob's widow. He knew he couldn't bring back Rob, but he could at least make sure the woman his buddy left behind wasn't hiding from humanity for the rest of her life.

The lights flickered again and again, and the house turned dark. "Looks like you got the food ready just in time. Where do you keep your candles and flashlights?"

"In the kitchen," she muttered and he heard her stand.

"I can help."

"No, that's okay. Just guard my plate so the cat doesn't get my food."

He chuckled. "I can do that."

He heard her stumble around in the kitchen, bumping into things, opening and closing drawers. After a couple of minutes, he couldn't stand it anymore and he picked up both plates and carefully walked into the kitchen.

"I'm right behind you," he murmured, not wanting her to back into him and upset the plates.

She gave a squeak of surprise and he successfully avoided her then set the plates on the counter.

"Matches," she said. "I can't find the matches. They should be in this drawer."

"Let me try," he said, finding her arm with his hand and following it to the drawer. Some part of him was reluctant to trade the smooth sensation of her skin for the articles in the drawer, but he did. His hand brushed hers in the search for the matches and he felt an odd sensual thrill. He heard her catch her breath and wondered if she felt it, too. His fingers closed around a small rectangular cardboard object. "Got it. Where are your flashlights anyway?"

"Bedroom," she said.

"Ah, to ward off the aliens under the bed."

"Right. I've got the candle right here."

Brock struck the match, lighting it on the first try, and quickly lit the candle. He looked at the soft light illuminating Callie's features and felt a warmth grow in his belly. "You look like an angel." The words spilled out impulsively and he immediately felt self-conscious.

"It's the candlelight. Everyone looks angelic."

"Not me," he said dryly.

She smiled. "Maybe a dark angel."

"That's a stretch."

She laughed. "Here," she said, putting the wick of another candle against the lit one. It hit him that this was what some people did during wedding ceremonies. Alarm rushed through him. Now that was just too weird.

"I'll go get the flashlights now."

She returned with the flashlights and a battery-operated radio. "Good girl," he said.

"I may seem like an unprepared flake, but I'm not. We'd better finish eating before the food gets cold."

Finishing before she did, he messed with the radio and found an AM station where the deejay reported massive blackouts. The electric company warned that power might not return until morning.

"Oh, goody," she muttered. "I guess I won't be working tonight."

"Do you have any cards?"

"Somewhere. I haven't played in a while."

"I thought you might like to try to beat me at James Bond Junior."

She gave a double take. "I always beat Rob at James Bond Junior."

"But can you beat me?"

She lifted an eyebrow. "We'll have to see."

He won the first two games and she was not at all happy. The way she fumed reminded him of a buzzing honey bee.

"I demand a rematch. Those first two games were flukes."

"Flukes?" he echoed, enjoying taunting her just a little. "You're just peeved because I'm beating the pants off of you."

"My pants are staying exactly where they are," she retorted. "You're the one who's still not dressed. That's your secret weapon."

"What *are* you talking about?"

"Your chest. It's distracting. That's why you're winning. You play dirty."

He brushed her backhanded compliment aside, although he felt flattered as hell. "I wouldn't call it dirty," he said. "I just always play to win. You want to go again?"

She met his gaze and he saw her bite her lip as she glanced at his chest then back to his face. Her expression was shockingly hungry and sexual. He immediately turned hard. He wanted to bring her small artist's hand to his chest and feel her touch. He wanted to take that plump lip she was biting with his mouth and tongue. He wanted to slide his hands over the wonderland of her body and feel every inch of her skin against every inch of his. Then he wanted to sink himself so deep inside her—

"Go again," she said in a husky voice. "I'll win this time."

The game began and he heard her breath and inhaled her scent. With every flip of the cards, he felt himself grow hotter. The image of her hair hanging around his face like a curtain, skimming over his bare skin, down his belly. He told himself to stop, but his body spurred his mind on. He wanted her small breasts in his mouth. He wanted to be inside her where it was warm and good.

"James Bond Junior," she said triumphantly. "I told you I would win."

"So you did," he said.

"What do you want to do now?"

"Nothing, I ought to—" he muttered under his breath.

"Pardon? I didn't hear you."

"Nothing," he said, moving his tight shoulders. It felt like his entire body was stretched tight. He suddenly felt her hand over his and his heart stopped.

"Brock?"

"Yeah?"

"If I ask you a question, would you answer it with the truth?"

His heart started beating again, way too fast. Her hand felt like a branding iron and he grit his teeth to keep from turning his palm over and pulling her to him. "What is this? Truth or dare now?"

"Just truth. Why did you come to see me?"

He sighed, conflicted. "Why do you ask?"

"Because I want to know."

"He was afraid you would turn into a hermit if something happened to him."

She made a sound of disgust and jerked her hand away. "I haven't become a hermit. I've been independent. I even moved to the beach. I always told him I'd wanted to live at the beach."

He raked his hand through his hair. If they were going down this road, then he was going to make her face the truth. "How many people have you met since you moved here?"

"My landlord and a boy who was looking for his dog," she said defensively.

"Callie, you haven't even spent more than thirty minutes in a grocery store. You're white as a ghost because you sleep all day and work at night."

"Maybe I'm part vampire," she joked.

She was sucking the restraint out of him. "You've done what Rob was afraid you would do. You've become a hermit. You haven't made any friends. You haven't gotten involved with anything or anyone. You've cut yourself off from the rest of the world."

"I have not. It's just taking me a while to find my—" She broke off as if she couldn't find the word.

"What? Your mojo?"

She snorted. "I never had a mojo."

"That's a matter of opinion."

She stared at him. "What do you mean?"

"You've obviously got some kind of mojo going with your art," he said with a shrug. "And I'm sure there are plenty of men, given the opportunity," he added meaningfully, "who would like to help you explore your mojo."

"I don't want anyone but Rob," she whispered, and the pain in her eyes chipped at his heart.

"I know, but he wants you to go on. He wouldn't want you to live this way."

She closed her eyes. "I can't love anyone."

Unable to keep himself from touching her, he took her hand in his. "If ever someone was made to love, it was you, Callie. I could have told you that just by looking at the photo Rob kept of you."

"But how do you love when you don't feel like living?" she asked him, opening her eyes to search his.

"You wake up every morning and you put one foot in front of the other. You go through the motions until you start to feel again, and you will."

She took a careful breath. "So your coming here was a pity call, after all."

He shook his head. "You've got your pain. I've got

my demons. I can't help thinking I should have been the one to die."

She turned her head away from him and he had the odd sensation of the sun turning its back on him. He couldn't blame her if she thought he should have been the one to die instead of Rob.

She turned back to him, lifting her chin. "Rob wouldn't want you to be thinking that way, would he?"

He let out a breath he hadn't known he'd been holding. "No, Rob was a great guy," he said. *And I want his wife so bad I can taste it.*

Four

Marine Lingo Translation
RON: Remain Overnight

"I'm an introvert. I was born an introvert. What if I don't want to be friendly and meet new people?" Callie argued as they took a fast walk on the beach the next morning.

After her electricity finally came on near midnight, Brock returned to his cottage, downed a beer, willed his brain not to think and fell asleep. His Marine conditioning was unforgiving, however, and he'd awakened early. After a run on the beach, he read the newspaper and visited Callie to coax her out for a walk.

The sun shone like diamonds on the water while the tide washed over the beat-up beach. "You have to make yourself. You need to meet new people whether you want to or not."

Her jaw tightened and she frowned. "I shouldn't have to if I don't want to."

"That's a selfish attitude," Brock said bluntly.

Her eyes rounded and she stopped dead in her tracks. "I'm not selfish. I'm just not outgoing. I'm more comfortable by myself."

He stopped, squaring off with her. She was probably going to think he was a nut, but he could speak from experience. He didn't totally understand it, but looking at her photograph when he'd been overseas had given him a little lift even though he'd never really met her. "Did you ever think that there are some people who could benefit from knowing you? Did it ever occur to you that there could be people on this planet who need you in some way? People you haven't ever met?"

She blinked and stared at him for a long moment. "No. Why would anyone need me?"

Brock swallowed an oath. He could give her a thousand reasons. "For starters, there's your art. Those pictures you draw impact a lot of kids and parents. Those people are counting on you."

She squinted her eyes against the sun. "I guess I can see that. But I still don't see why I have to go out and meet people. I can just stay in my cottage and draw."

"Yeah, that's worked out real well the last several months, hasn't it?"

She shot him a dirty look and began to walk again. "That wasn't nice."

He shrugged. "May not be nice, but it's true. You've said you're not happy with what you've created."

"I'm recovering from my husband's death," she said, nearly spitting the words at him.

"You could spend your whole life recovering."

"I may just do that," she retorted.

He caught her by the arm. "You can't cut yourself off like this. Rob didn't want it."

"Well, Rob didn't get what he wanted and I didn't get what I wanted, either." She closed her eyes. "I don't want to feel anymore. I don't want to feel sad. I don't deserve to feel hap—" She broke off and opened her eyes.

Brock's heart clenched in his chest at the lost expression in her eyes. "You have to," he said. "You're gonna laugh. You're gonna cry. You're still alive, Callie. You may even love again."

She shook her head vigorously. "Even if I found someone, I wouldn't want to. It just hurts too much to lose."

He nodded. "Well, you're one up on me there. I haven't lost anyone except my father. I never had anything special with a woman."

"Was that because of you or the women?"

"I don't know," he said with a shrug. "Maybe I scare all the good girls with hearts and attract the bad girls like mosquitoes."

A chuckle bubbled from her throat. A reluctant

one, he thought, looking into her eyes. "Mosquitoes?" she echoed. "Bloodsuckers. Not the most flattering description of your past girlfriends."

"Girlfriend may be elevating the position." He nodded and snagged her wrist. "C'mon, let's keep walking."

"I'm starting to get the impression that I'm a how-to project for you."

"That's not all bad," he said lightly. "I've been commended for developing strategies that achieve goals."

"But what if your goal and mine are different?"

"Then we'll negotiate," he lied.

She looked at him skeptically. "You don't strike me as a particularly flexible kind of guy."

"Maybe I'll surprise you," he said, determined to keep the exchange light. If she knew what he really had planned, his life just might be in danger.

"You already have surprised me," she said darkly.

An impulse he couldn't ignore bit at him and he whisked her up into his arms.

She gasped, squirming in his arms. Her body felt soft and warm. "What are you doing?"

He carried her swiftly to the ocean as she started to kick and scream so loudly the seagulls squawked and flew away. Despite her struggle, he couldn't remember holding a woman who felt so sweet.

"What are you doing?" she demanded.

He kept walking and lowered both of them up to their shoulders into the cool water. She shrieked again and shook her head at him. With all her huffing and puffing, her breath played over him like a little breeze. "Why did you do that? The water's cold from the storm. I'm all wet."

"I am, too."

"So?" she said frowning.

"Think of it as a demonstration," he told her. "If my strategy gets you wet, I'll get wet, too."

She opened her mouth and her jaw worked, but no sound came out. Her eyebrows knit together. "I think you may be insane," she said.

He *knew* he was insane. He wanted to run his hands over all her curves and secret places. He was burning with need. Just having her in his arms was incredible temptation. Yep, he was definitely insane.

"I have no idea what your point is."

Sighing, he stood up and carried her from the ocean. "You'll understand soon enough," he said as he reluctantly set her down on the sand. He didn't want her to know he was hard. She would think he was a pervert.

Her teeth chattered and her nipples puckered against her tank top. "I don't like being told what's best for me."

It took all the self-discipline Brock possessed to lift his gaze from her small breasts. "As soon as you realize what's best for you, then nobody will need to tell you."

She scowled and turned away from him. "I'm a grown woman. I don't need you telling me what to do."

"Start acting like it then," he dared her.

She did a double take. "What do you mean?"

"I mean start acting like a grown woman."

She crossed her arms over her chest and gave him a long, considering glance. "I don't agree with your methods, but you may be kinda right."

"Kinda?" he asked.

"Okay, mostly. I probably should start acting like a grown woman, a live grown woman."

He nodded. "Yep."

She took a deep breath and nodded. "Yep. Even if it kills me."

Or kills me, he thought, as he watched her turn and treat him to the inviting sight of her backside encased in nearly transparent white shorts. Her underwear looked like it was a light lilac color. Brock felt himself harden again and groaned. If this was supposed to be the cure for his ravaged conscience, he wondered if boiling himself in water would be easier.

"I think you should start by going to a bar," Brock said that evening. He'd always been told the best way to get over a woman was to go to a bar, drink too many beers and meet a new woman. He figured the reverse would be true for Callie.

Looking at him as if he'd lost his mind, she shook her head. "No. That's like stealing home before you go to first, second or third base. I thought a nice quiet trip to the library—"

He shook his head. "Nope. Too solitary. The objective is to get you back and involved with *humans*, not books."

She made a face and sighed. "I agree that I need to get out more, to try to have more of a life, if for no other reason than my art. You're right. I've isolated myself. But I want to take it slowly at first. There's this cute little restaurant that serves all these different kinds of teas—"

Brock rolled his eyes. For Pete's sake, punitive night drills during boot camp had been easier than this. They negotiated for another five minutes and finally decided on a trip to the grocery store.

"Pitiful," he muttered under his breath as she pushed the cart through the produce section. "Pitiful."

"Hey, don't knock it. This is the first time I've been to a real grocery store in ages. You have to crawl before you can walk. Oh, look. Fresh peaches. I love fresh peaches."

"I know," Brock said and chuckled when she stuck out her tongue at him.

"Okay, smarty-pants, what's your favorite fruit?"

"Cherries," he said.

"No surprise there," she said dryly. "Given your way with the ladies."

He dropped his jaw in mock surprise. "I'm shocked that your mind would sink so low. My mother baked a great cherry pie. I usually had cherry pie for my birthday instead of cake. And my grandmother had a cherry tree in her backyard."

"Oops. Sorry. It was a natural connection to

make—cherries, ladies." Her cheeks bloomed. "Or not. Tell me about this pie your mother used to make. Did she make the crust from scratch? I never could figure out how to make a good crust."

He nodded, swallowing his humor over her chatty effort to cover her gaffe. "She made the whole thing from scratch. I have the recipe and I can make it."

Her eyes widened in disbelief. "You're kidding. You can bake a cherry pie from scratch?"

"Yeah. What's so unbelievable about that?"

She shrugged her shoulders. "You just don't seem the domestic type."

"I'm not, but I don't like to starve. And I don't get home much anymore, so if I want hot cherry pie, I make it myself."

She studied him. "You really don't get along with your stepfather, do you?"

"Tough relationship. I've accepted it."

"I bet your mom misses you, though."

He nodded, thinking how frequently she'd written him when he'd been in the hospital.

"Maybe you should go see her," she said.

He wasn't accustomed to women giving him advice about his mother. "Maybe I will after I get settled in Atlanta."

They turned the cart onto the dairy aisle and she picked up a couple of cartons of yogurt and a small jug of milk. "I could never live in Atlanta. Too busy. Too crowded. Too much traffic."

"Depends on your point of view. There's a lot of stimulation in Atlanta, lots of things to do."

"As an artist, I prefer the quiet of a smaller town."

"One of the things I learned as a Marine was to create the quiet inside me. That way, I take it with me wherever I go. I'm not dependent on my environment."

She looked at him thoughtfully. "I never thought of it that way."

They continued through the store and completed her shopping. One more aisle to go and it was the cookie aisle. "Are you going to be a good girl and avoid the sweets?"

"Absolutely not," she said, grabbing a box of cookies. He grinned. "For such a little thing, you sure like your sweets."

"High metabolism," she said and grabbed one more box. "That's all," she said, but stopped suddenly near the end of the aisle.

"What is it?" he asked, seeing her features tighten with pain.

She held her breath. "It's silly, really silly. But he loved animal crackers. Even when he grew up, Rob loved animal crackers. I sent them to him when he was overseas."

Brock felt a sharp twist in his chest at the lost expression on Callie's face. She and Rob had known each other for so long that there would be many memories that would ambush her at odd times. It occurred to him that she might feel barraged with those memories when she ventured outside her cottage.

"Breathe," he said. "It's worse when you freeze up."

She glanced at him in surprise and took a shallow breath.

"Take another one, deeper," he coached, and watched her make the effort. He reached across her and took the small box of animal crackers from the shelf.

"Why did you—"

"We're going to eat these in Rob's memory," he said.

He drove her back to the cottage and they unloaded her groceries. She pulled out the box of animal crackers, opened it and solemnly ate a lion. She offered Brock a giraffe. She munched on a monkey then swallowed.

"This is probably very disrespectful to mention at this particular moment, but—" She lowered her voice to a whisper. "I don't like animal crackers."

Brock chuckled. "Neither do I. They taste like cardboard."

She smiled. "Rob must've liked them because his mother got them for him."

"That's possible. You know me and cherry pie."

Her eyes sparkled. "Yeah. For me, it's chocolate chip cookies. Great big, fat, hot cookies loaded—and I mean loaded—with chocolate chips."

Her voice was husky with a sexy indulgence that made his blood race to his crotch. He bit back an oath. Just hearing her talk about a cookie made him hard.

Callie closed the box and put it in the cabinet. "I'll save these for someone else."

"Just make sure you don't leave them in there until they're museum quality."

She laughed. "Duly noted. I think I'd like to play some music. Do you mind? It's a nice evening. Would you like some lemonade to wash down the cardboard?"

"Sure," he said, accepting the glass she offered and wandering out onto the patio. The sensual sound of a song by the artist Seal eased through the speakers of her stereo. In another situation, he would be drinking a beer or a glass of wine and getting his date ready for some time between the sheets. Instead he'd eaten animal crackers, was drinking lemonade, and was probably going to be taking a cold shower when he returned to his cottage tonight. The irony was sweet, he thought, shaking his head.

He heard Callie step onto the patio behind him. She sighed. "I need to thank you," she said in a low voice.

"Why?" he asked, turning to look at her. Her hair was pale in the moonlight, her eyes glowed with mystery. Looking at her made something inside him twist and something else inside him ease all at the same time.

"It's embarrassing to admit, but I realized it at the grocery store. It's like I've been totally locked up. Can't breathe, can't eat," she said with a lopsided smile. "Well, can't eat much anyway. Can't sleep. Can't do much of anything." She took a deep breath. "Breathing is a good place to start."

She was so charming with her vulnerability. He

wanted to pull her in his arms and tell her she would be okay, but he knew he shouldn't. He crammed his fists into his pockets.

"Thanks."

"No problem," he said and downed the rest of his lemonade. "Well, I should probably head back to my cottage."

"Do you have to?"

His heart stuttered at the expression in her eyes. "Why?"

She shrugged. "Sounds wussy, but I don't want to be alone yet tonight."

"Okay," he said, mentally girding himself for more sexual temptation—and deprivation. "What do you want to do?"

"Cards, Scrabble, Monopoly."

"Monopoly," he said decisively. If he couldn't have sex, he would dominate the real estate world.

An hour and a half later, she shook her head at him. "Whew! You're ruthless and you own everything," she complained. "I can't land on anything where I don't have to pay you rent. And I'm nearly broke. How'd you get to be so good?"

"This was how I got kisses when I was thirteen," he said, rolling the dice. "I played with a couple of neighbor girls. They always ended up owing me and I allowed them to pay some of their rent in trade."

"You dirty dog," she said. "You started young. Well, I'm not trading my kisses to pay your obscene rent."

"I hadn't asked," he said lightly, even though he felt himself go tight inside.

"That's right. You haven't," she said, meeting his gaze with a hint of curiosity in her eyes. That curiosity did dangerous things to his gut. She bit her lip. "I'm not at all your type."

He nodded and glanced away, focusing on moving his token. "Yep."

"You prefer uncommitted, undemanding, sexually experienced women with healthy appetites," she continued.

"You hit the nail on the head," he said, telling himself it was the truth. *Why did it feel like a lie?*

"Do you dance?"

He blinked and looked at her. "What?"

Her smile was a little self-conscious. "Do you dance?"

He nodded. "Yeah. Why?"

"Rob didn't."

"Really? I didn't know that, but then I never asked him to dance."

She laughed and then the silence stretched between them. His heart picked up the pace. He tried to ignore it, tried to ignore the expectant tension between them, tried not to think about holding her in his arms for a few moments. No kissing, no making love, just a dance. She hadn't gotten that from Rob. Maybe he wouldn't mind. The words were out before he could stop them.

"Wanna dance?"

Five

Marine Lingo Translation
Cinderella Liberty: An authorized absence that
expires at midnight.

He took her small hand in his and pulled her into
his arms. She slid her other hand over his shoulder then behind his back as he drew her closer. She
fit against him as if she were made for his body.
Made for his soul, something inside him whispered. Brock stopped himself. *What crazy
thoughts*. He inhaled and caught a draft of the
sweet, citrus scent of her hair. He felt the silky
strands brush his chin.

Her breasts glanced his rib cage and his abdomen
tightened. Her thighs slid against his and his heart
pounded.

He tried to swallow the knot of need forming in

his throat. The song playing on the radio would have provided a perfect accompaniment to a long French kiss or an afternoon spent in bed. It was slow and sexy, not the kind of music for twirling.

He cleared his throat, needing to break the tension, the magic. "Who is this artist? I don't think I've heard him before."

"I can tell you've been out of the country," she said with soft amusement in her voice. "John Mayer. He's very popular."

"Do you like him?"

He felt her nod. "Yes. His voice is expressive, so are his lyrics."

It would be so easy to rub his lips over her forehead, Brock thought. So easy. She might not even notice. He gave in to the temptation and a surge of illicit pleasure raced through him. He swallowed an oath at the strength of it. If kissing her forehead did this to him, then what would kissing her other places do to him?

Brock closed his eyes and tried to close his mind to all the possibilities. She just probably needed a little human contact. A brotherly hug. He shouldn't think about nudging her chin upward and tasting her mouth, or sliding his hand down to her bottom to draw her against the part of him that grew harder with each breath she took.

He heard her murmur something and opened his eyes. "What'd you say?"

Feeling her pull her head back slightly, he looked

down at her. A strand of her hair clung to his chin. Pulling it free, she smiled and lifted her fingers to his chin. "Five o'clock shadow. Rob must have been jealous of you. I think he had about ten whiskers on his face and three hairs on his chest."

Fighting a twinge of self-consciousness, Brock rubbed his jaw. "I've always had to shave often or—"

"Or you get scrubby."

"Yeah," he said and noticed that her gaze fell to his chest. It was a little thing, but it grabbed at his gut. She was aware of him as a man, perhaps just because of his beard, but the awareness was there. He could see it and feel it. All of his instincts pushed him to take this further, to lower his mouth to hers and rub his hands over every inch of her body.

His conscience jabbed at him. He would be taking unfair advantage. Unfair advantage of Rob's wife. Of Rob.

Clenching his jaw, he pulled back. "Song's over," he muttered.

This would have been so much easier if Callie was a guy. He could pat her on the back, watch some baseball games on television with her, go to a bar, help her pick up somebody so she could get laid. After that, if she were a guy, she'd be as good as new.

Guys were simpler than women. Sports, beer and a good lay could solve a lot of problems. Women, however, were much more complicated. And Callie was no exception. During his training, he'd been taught that in order to defeat the enemy, he needed to understand the way the enemy thought. Callie wasn't the enemy, but he sure as hell didn't think the same way she did. He racked his brain for a way to pull her out of her slump and even resorted to something he'd never done before—he called the one woman he could trust for advice.

"Hey, Mom, how's everything?"

"Brock! I wondered where you'd gone. I called the rehab center and no one knew. I was worried sick—"

Brock winced. He'd been in such a rush to leave he'd forgotten to tell her. "Sorry, Mom. I'd had enough. I had to get out of there. I decided I needed a change of environment before I moved to Atlanta."

"So where are you?"

"Down in South Carolina. It's a little place on the beach."

"Oh, the ocean," his mother said longingly. "That sounds nice."

"Yeah, you should get Sam to take you sometime. Listen, I was thinking about you the other day."

"That's sweet of you to say, dear. You know I think of you all the time. Sam and I miss you terribly. We were hoping you would come see us when you left the rehab center."

Brock felt a pinch of discomfort. "I was thinking about trying to get up to see you after I get settled in Atlanta. I'll have a lot to do. But I was thinking about when Dad died. I was wondering how you kept it all together. I remember catching you crying a few times, but you didn't ever fall apart."

Silence followed. "Well, that was because of you, Brock. If it had been left up to me, I would have curled into a ball and never left the house. I was lost without your father. But I still had my precious son and I needed to be strong for you."

Brock's heart tightened at the memory. He remembered that period of time just after his father's death. He'd been confused and lost, but his mother had seemed so strong. He was surprised to learn how hard it had been for her. "You did a good job, Mom. I didn't know."

She sighed. "Everyone needs a reason to get up in the morning. You were mine," she said, and he heard the smile in her voice. "When someone close to you dies, it's a struggle to go on, but you just have to. You have to get up, get dressed and go out in the world. Sometimes it's little things that help. Smelling flowers, holding a baby, striking up a conversation with someone you don't know. And for women, shopping can be a panacea, even if we don't buy anything. I remember going shopping twice a week after your father died. I didn't usually buy anything, but it got me out among people. And then I joined a garden club and got a job. And when I met Sam, I thought he could be a good father for you."

She didn't sound too sure with that last reference to his stepfather. "He was in a tough position," Brock conceded.

"And you're both bullheaded," his mother said.

"True. Maybe that's why you love us both so much," he said.

She laughed with pleasure and the sound pleased him. "You've always been a rascal. Are you taking care of yourself? Eating good food? Taking your vitamins and getting your rest?"

"Yes, Mom," he said, stifling a groan.

"Don't you *yes, Mom* me," she fussed. "We nearly lost you, so I'm allowed to worry."

"You didn't lose me. I'm still ornery as ever."

"So when will you come to see me?"

"Soon. Two or three months."

"Promise?"

"Promise. Thanks, Mom."

"Anytime, dear. Take care of yourself."

"You, too," he said and hung up the phone.

He thought back to the conversation and made a mental list of what his mother had said. *Smelling flowers, joining clubs, getting a job, shopping.* He wrinkled his nose in distaste at the last activity, and Callie already had a job. He would try the others first.

Brock didn't know much about flowers, so he got two of each, along with a couple of big pots, some bags of dirt and gardening tools. After he hauled everything onto Callie's front porch, he rang the doorbell.

She answered more quickly than ever, and she actually looked as if she'd been awake for a while. His heart lifted at the sight of her. Her hair was pulled back in some kind of messy bun. He wished she would wear it down. Her legs looked lean and shapely despite her loose shorts.

Glancing at the flowers for a long moment, she finally met his gaze. "Just a guess, but I'm thinking Rob didn't tell you that I have a black thumb."

"He told me you don't have a black thumb. You just get distracted and forget to water plants."

She crossed her arms over her chest. "Well, they're not like pets. They don't remind you to give them water—until it's too late."

"I have a solution for that," he said.

"What?" she asked skeptically.

"I'll tell you after we plant the flowers."

She gave a put-upon sigh, but joined him on the porch. "Is this part of my recovery?"

"Yes." He gave her a trowel and opened one of the bags of dirt.

"Where'd you get this idea?"

"My mother." He dumped some dirt into each of the large pots.

She looked at him with her eyebrows raised. "Your mother? I didn't know you ever talked with your mother."

Brock resisted the urge to growl. "What is it with women? All or nothing. I call my mother every now and then. I even wrote her when I was overseas and when I was in the physical rehabilitation center. I called her last night and—"

"Bet she was surprised," Callie interjected.

Brock shot her a quelling glance that didn't appear to dent her challenging, impish expression.

"Betcha she was surprised," she said, shaking her trowel at him. "Betcha she didn't even know where you were calling her from."

"And your point is?"

She wiggled the trowel in a circle as if she were trying to come up with something, but couldn't. "Nothing really, except you don't call her as often as she'd like. Did you talk about me?"

"No. I just asked her what she did to keep going when my dad died."

The silence that stretched between them had a sweet quality to it. He glanced up and saw sympathy in her gaze. He usually hated the very idea of someone feeling sympathy for him, especially after all his time in the hospital, but it felt different coming from Callie. He would have to figure that out later.

"That must've been a rough time for both of you," she said.

He nodded. "It was. I don't think I realized how tough it was for her until lately."

"So how did she get through? Gardening?" Callie asked with a smile on her face. She shifted one of the flowers into the larger pot.

"That and some other things," he said.

"Do I have these other things to look forward to?" she asked warily.

"Some. Not all," he said, thinking that the way she looked at him with her hair partly covering one eye was sexy as all get-out.

"What won't I be doing?"

He felt a ripple of discomfort. "Well, you don't have a kid, so…"

She met his gaze again, realization glinting through her eyes. "Yeah, I can see that. I bet you were her biggest motivation for getting up in the morning."

"I guess that's what mothers are supposed to say."

She smiled. "I never have understood why guys hate having their moms fuss over them a little."

"Because it's never a little. It starts out small and innocent with her fixing my favorite pie, then it progresses to grilling me about my health, fussing over me eating vegetables, then before you know it, she's trying to pick out a wife for me and begging for grandchildren."

"And by then, you're choking on your cherry pie," she said, chuckling. "How are we going to arrange these flowers?"

He shrugged. "You're the artist."

"With a black thumb," she added.

"Okay, these are annuals," he said, pointing to the flowers next to him. "The ones next to you are perennials. So some of them will come back again next year and some of them won't."

"Kinda like you," she murmured.

He could have let it pass, but he was curious. He set down his trowel. "How are they like me?"

"The annuals are pretty for a season, but they won't be back next year."

"Are you saying I'm pretty?" he teased.

"I'm saying you're temporary," she emphasized, and he couldn't tell if she was saying it more for him or for herself. "Then again," she said, instantly lightening the mood with a rueful smile. "They may *all* be temporary due to my black thumb."

He shook his head. "This time is gonna be different. The annuals will last all season and the perennials will be back next year."

If he couldn't be here with her next spring, then at least the damn flowers would, he thought. *Now that was insane. Purely insane. Why did he give a rip if these flowers bloomed next year?* And he sure didn't want to be here next year wanting another man's woman and not having her.

Insisting she wasn't a joiner, Callie didn't bite at the club suggestion, even after he read a list compiled by the local newspaper. He subscribed to the local paper for her, figuring it would be worth the cost if she read the comics and just one of them made her smile.

When he knocked on her door one afternoon, she answered with a pink nose, pink cheeks and tearful eyes. His gut clenched. "What's wrong?"

"This isn't a good day," she said in a wobbly voice. "I don't think I'm going to be very good company. You'd probably better go back to your place."

"I'm not going back to my place. What is it?"

She bit her lip. "It's his birthday," she whispered. "It's Rob's birthday. I've spent nearly every birthday with him since he was ten."

His chest tightened at the pain he saw in her eyes. She looked like a lost child. Unable to stop himself, he pulled her into his arms and she sobbed against him. She sniffled and snorted and wept. "I'm sorry. I'm really sorry. I told you that you should go back—"

"Hush," he said, holding her tighter. "This is why I'm here."

She inhaled deeply and let it out in a jagged, uneven breath.

He stroked her hair the same way he would comfort a child, all the while aware—terribly aware—that she was a woman. "Does this mean we have to eat the animal crackers in his honor?"

She gave a weak chuckle and looked up at him. "No. He didn't usually have animal crackers on his birthday. Just the regular birthday cake, yellow cake, white frosting, candles." She rubbed the tears from her cheeks. "Sorry."

"It's okay. What do you want to do this evening?"

"I don't know. Maybe look at some photographs. I'd toast him, but I don't think I have any alcohol."

"I can take care of that," he offered.

She took a step back and shook her head. "Oh, no. You can't stay. This is really going to be maudlin and I'll just keep this to myself."

He immediately felt the gap where she'd been. "Are you saying I'm not invited?"

She opened her mouth and worked it, but nothing came out. "Well, it's not going to be a fun time."

"I miss him, too," he confessed.

She looked at him for a long moment. "Okay. You can come to my pity party if you really want to."

"Let me go pick up something for toasting first," he said, pointing at her. "I'll be back in a flash. Don't start without me."

She shrugged. "Whatever you say."

Twenty-two minutes later, he returned with tequila, salt, lime, a birthday cake and two shot glasses.

She raised her eyebrows at his purchase. "That looks like an interesting taste combination."

"After you drink a couple shots, your taste buds will be numb and it won't matter."

She gave a weak laugh. "That's good to know."

Brock washed out the glasses and sliced the lime while she cut a couple pieces of cake. "Where's the party?"

"The den," she said, licking the frosting from one of her fingers.

"I'm ready when you are," he said and followed her out of the kitchen.

Crossing her legs over each other, she set the pieces of cake aside and picked up a large photo album. "Let's start with the first birthday. He was cute even when he was a baby."

"He was," Brock agreed, seeing the same sparkle in the baby's eyes that he'd seen in Rob's eyes.

"He walked early and loved anything on wheels," she continued.

"Yep, he got a kick out of the vehicles the Marines used."

"He drove a motorcycle before he was old enough to get his driver's license, but he didn't get caught." She shook her head. "He never got caught."

Except when he stepped on that mine. He got caught then. Brock's chest contracted so sharply he couldn't breathe. He shook some salt on his hand, licked it, poured a shot of tequila, downed it and sucked on a lime.

He felt Callie's gaze on him. "That always looked like it required a lot of coordination to me."

"You've never had tequila?"

"That would require me going to a bar, and the only times I went to bars I was with Rob. He always got me one of those drinks with the little umbrellas."

"You want to try a shot?" he asked.

"Okay, but you'll have to coach me," she said.

Brock talked her through the salt and the shot and watched her face after she tossed back the tequila. "Ewww. That's gross!" She coughed.

"Suck the lime," he told her, lifting her hand.

She obeyed and her lips puckered and eyes watered. She coughed again. He gently thumped her on her back.

"That's disgusting. Why would anyone drink more than one of those?" she asked in a hoarse voice.

After viewing several more pages of photographs of Rob, however, she took another shot when Brock did. She shared memory after memory with Brock. Some were funny, some were bittersweet, but they all made him ache because she obviously missed him so much. It hit him again that Callie hadn't just lost a lover or husband—she'd lost her life partner. And nothing, and no one, would ever be able to totally replace everything Rob had been to her.

The knowledge tore at him and he felt his own eyes burn when she turned the page to show Rob in his uniform, fresh out of boot camp.

Callie scrubbed at her eyes with the backs of her hands and took another shot. "I think I'm starting to feel the effect of the tequila now. I should probably eat something," she said. "Cake. I'll eat the cake."

"I'm not sure that's really gonna help," he said, amused, despite the fact that she'd been weeping like a child just moments before.

"Better than nothing," she said and took a couple of bites.

He watched her and got distracted by the little bit of frosting on her cheek. He rubbed it off with his finger then licked it.

Her gaze locked with his in fascination. "After this cake, I bet that tequila will taste more bitter than ever."

"You bet right," he said with a grin.

She sighed and took another bite of cake. "Well, I can say that I did something adventurous on Rob's birthday by trying tequila."

"Hear, hear," he said, pouring himself another shot. "And you can feel good that you didn't do anything too bad, like body slammers."

She swallowed over her bite of cake. "What's a body slammer?"

"Nothing you want to do," he told her. A dozen forbidden images flew through his mind of places on her body he would like to taste.

She leaned toward him with her hand on his thigh. She probably didn't even realize she was touching him, he thought. "Tell me what a body slammer is," she demanded.

Her eyes were sexy, smoky and her voice had a husky tinge that rattled his nerve endings. "It's when you put salt on another person's body, lick it off, drink the shot of tequila and follow it up with the lime." His brain ran down the road to temptation again.

She blinked. "Now let me get this straight. You pour salt on someone else's body and lick it off. Doesn't it just fall off?"

"You have to do it fast."

She was quiet for a long moment. "I can honestly say I've never had a body slammer."

Brock felt a punch of arousal along with an uh-oh sensation. She had that same look on her face she'd worn when he'd danced with her. That one little dance had nearly killed him. He would swallow his tongue before he offered her a body slammer.

She bit her lip and eyed the tequila then her gaze slid over him again. She'd had enough alcohol to lower her inhibitions, which could be a damn dangerous state for him. Her expectancy was so palpable, it twisted between them like a coiled wire. "I really don't know when I'm going to have this opportunity again," she said and licked her lips. "And I can trust you. If I don't choose anything obscene, would you let me body slam you?"

Six

Marine Lingo Translation
Devil Dog: a name for Marines that signifies
the dogged determination of Marines.

*And I can trust you...would you let me body slam
you?*

Brock swallowed every swear word he'd ever
heard along with a few he made up. *She could trust
him? She damn well shouldn't trust him.* He felt like
the biggest, baddest wolf on the planet and he wanted
this Little Red Riding Hood for breakfast, lunch and
dinner.

Squeezing in a breath, he willed his lips to form
the word *no,* all the while looking into her sexy eyes.
He glanced at her mouth and felt his libido roar like
an overbuilt engine.

"Go ahead," he said, his voice sounding rough to his own ears. "Body slam me."

Her face lit up and she smiled. "Okay, I'll try it on your hand." She poured her shot then grabbed the salt shaker and sprinkled some on the back of his hand. Leaning forward, she lowered her mouth and stuck out her tongue. She started to laugh and backed away. "Sorry," she said. "This is just one of the most bizarre things I've done in a long time."

Her laughter was as seductive as everything else about her. Brock was amused and aroused. Unbearably so.

She pressed two fingers over her mouth as if to force herself to stop giggling. "I can do this. I want to be able to say I've body slammed."

Lowering her head again, she leaned forward and slid her tongue over his skin. The sight and sensation of her pink tongue on his flesh tightened every cell inside him. She rubbed her tongue from side to side and he felt his temperature rise with every stroke. *Damn, she was just licking his hand. What if she'd been licking his...*

She pulled back and a groan escaped his throat. She tossed back the tequila with a grimace and quickly followed by sucking on another slice of lime. "Well, that was interesting," she said with a smile.

"I think you've had enough," he said, tossing back one more shot himself.

"Maybe," she said. "How many have I—"

"One clue that you've had enough is when you can't remember how many you drank."

She moved her head in a circle. "Are you gonna body slam me?"

She had no idea how much he wanted to body slam her—and his idea of body slamming had nothing to do with tequila.

"Fair's fair," she said, lifting her hand.

Unable to resist, he poured another shot and got his lime ready then sprinkled salt on her and lowered his head.

She started to giggle and the salt fell off. "It tickled."

Caught somewhere between agonizing arousal and amusement, he laughed. "Give me your hand," he said and turned her wrist over. Holding it steady, he sprinkled salt on the inside of her wrist and lowered his mouth to her skin.

Her soft intake of breath was like an intimate touch. He slid his tongue over the inside of her wrist, savoring the flavor and texture of her skin mixed with the salt. He licked the tiny blue vein beneath her fair skin.

"Oh, my," she whispered.

Reluctantly pulling back, he tossed back the shot and sucked the lime. She looked at him with a mixture of curiosity and sensual wariness, as if he were some wild animal she should avoid but found fascinating, all the same.

"That's some drink. A body slammer. I think I better get a drink of water." She stood and lifted her hand to her head. "Whew! I feel wobbly."

Brock caught her hand and tugged her back onto the couch. "Stay here. I'll get it."

"You had more tequila than I did. How come you aren't woozy like me?"

He stood. "Men metabolize alcohol faster than women do."

"But you didn't even eat any cake," she protested.

He went into the kitchen and filled two glasses with ice water, then returned. Still standing, he drank his water, hoping it would bring him a little sanity. He was tempted to pour the stuff over his head to cool himself down.

He felt Callie's gaze on him as she sipped her water. She patted the cushion beside her. "Would you stay a little longer? I don't want to be alone yet."

He sank down onto the sofa and felt the silence between them.

"Could I ask a favor of you?"

"Sure," he said, knowing there wasn't much she could ask that he wouldn't do.

"Would you hold me for a little while?"

His heart turned over at the vulnerability in her sweet features. "Sure," he said and pulled her into his arms. Her body was soft and pliable. She relaxed against him as if she had no idea how much he wanted to undress her and make love to her. She stuck her face against his throat and inhaled deeply then lifted her hands to his shoulders. Her hair felt like silk beneath his chin. His heart hammered in his chest while her breaths evened out and she drifted off to sleep.

Hours later, the low sound of a motor awakened him. Brock opened his eyes, immediately aware that Callie was spread over him like a blanket. Something gray moved beside him and he turned his head to see the cat. The cat, whose whiskers were covered in white frosting, stared at him unblinkingly and purred.

Brock shifted slightly, but Callie continued to sleep. He shifted again and, when she didn't move, he thought about putting a mirror under her nose to make sure she was breathing. The tequila must have delivered a knockout punch.

His body groaned in protest at the crumpled position he'd been in for the last several hours. He had an ugly suspicion his body was going to exact a heavy punishment. Grimacing, he carefully slid Callie off of him and onto another cushion on the couch. She stirred, but continued to sleep.

Rising from the couch, he stretched and felt pain shoot through his back and leg. His head throbbed. Yep, he probably shouldn't have downed that last shot of tequila. He took the remainder of the cake sitting on the table and tossed it in the trash in the kitchen. Returning to the den, he looked at Callie and felt his chest tighten. Her hair spilled over the dark upholstery, looking like wildfire. Her rosebud lips were slightly parted.

Lord, how he wanted her.

But he couldn't have her.

Heaving a sigh, he went to the sofa and carefully picked her up and carried her toward the back of the house, where he suspected her bedroom was.

"What are you doing?" she asked as he stepped through the doorway.

"Putting you to bed."

"What time is it?"

"Very late or very early, depending on your perspective," he said.

"My head feels like the hunchback of Notre Dame is ringing cathedral bells inside it."

"Yeah, I feel like crap, too."

"I feel dizzy when I open my eyes."

"Then keep them closed," he told her, and lowered her onto her bed. "I'm going to bring a glass of water and some aspirin and put it on your bedside table."

"Why?"

"If I don't, you may kill me in the morning," he muttered, and collected the items. He returned to the bedroom to find her under the sheet and tossing articles of her clothing on the floor. Her shirt flew through the air, followed by her bra and shorts.

His temperature climbed several degrees as his mind stripped down the covers to her bed and he found her naked, warm and waiting. Inviting.

"You can sleep on the sofa if you think you shouldn't be driving," she said.

Not exactly the invitation his libido had been wishing for. "That's okay. I'm gonna walk home."

Her eyes still closed, she frowned. "It's too late for that."

"Nah, the fresh air will do me good." Hopefully it would get his brain out of his shorts.

She sighed.

"Sit up just a little," he coaxed.

"I don't want to take anything. I'm too sleepy."

"You don't even have to open your eyes," he told her and she lifted her head slightly.

He touched her bottom lip and when she opened her mouth, he placed the aspirin on her tongue. He held the glass of water to her lips and she swallowed. After repeating the process, he lowered her head to the pillow. "Thanks, Brock. Did you know you taste a lot better than tequila?" she asked, tossing her panties over the edge of the bed and rolling onto her side.

Brock rubbed his hand over his face in frustration. *…you taste a lot better than tequila.* In any other situation, he would be in that bed and on her in three seconds flat. But not in this situation, he told himself. Not with this woman.

"I'm never drinking tequila again," Callie said as she opened her door to him the next morning. With her hair sticking out in no less than ten directions, she put her hands on either side of her face and shook her head. She wore a little robe and Brock suspected she was naked beneath it. The knowledge cranked up his body temperature.

"You didn't warn me that I would feel like my body had been slammed the next morning."

"I encouraged you to stop, but you wanted to continue," he pointed out, following her inside. "Are you ready for your run?"

She looked at him in disbelief. "What are you? The Terminator or something? Are you sure you aren't hiding steel underneath that skin?" Callie asked, poking at one of Brock's biceps.

He caught her finger and shook his head. "No steel. Just the regular combination of blood and guts."

"No way," she said. "You're not regular anything."

Her compliment felt like a soft stroke on his skin. He cracked a smile. "It's my Marine training. C'mon. Let's go. The fresh air will make you feel better."

Callie made a face. "A twelve-hour nap would make me feel better."

"Go get dressed," he told her.

"We're not really going to run, are we?"

"We'll take it easy," he promised.

She made another face. "Your version of easy and my version of easy are very, very different," she grumbled, but headed toward her bedroom. "Did you know Oscar got into the cake last night?" she yelled from the bedroom.

"Yeah, his purring was what woke me up."

"Who would have thought a cat would like birthday cake?"

He heard her walk from her bedroom to the bathroom, followed by the sounds of water and a little shriek. "Oh, my hair! I look like something out of a horror movie."

Chuckling at her dismay, he strolled closer to the hallway. "It wasn't that bad. You just looked like a wannabe rock star."

"Cute, very cute," she retorted and opened the door, her hair pulled back in a high ponytail and a scowl on her face. "This is really all your fault. Tequila."

He lifted his hands. "I encouraged you to stop."

"Hmmph. Okay, Dr. Torture, let's go."

They took a short jog on the beach and slowed to a walk after a short time. Callie wandered closer to the edge of the tide and looked out on the ocean. "I'll say one thing for how I feel today. I feel so cruddy physically that I can't focus on whining about Rob."

"You don't whine," Brock said as he joined her. "At least, not about Rob."

Her lips twitched. "You're so kind."

He shrugged. "Your grief is valid."

"Yeah, but I've made a full-time job of it. He wouldn't want it that way. Plus, it's exhausting and unproductive."

"So what are you going to do?"

She met his gaze. "I'm already *doing.* I've allowed myself to get suckered into the Brock Armstrong recovery program, haven't I?"

"Kicking and screaming every inch of the way."

She studied him. "I just wish you didn't feel like you had a penance to pay for surviving when Rob didn't."

Her words hit too close and he looked away. "It's more complicated than that."

"Okay. Whatever it is, thanks."

"It works both ways. Helping you helps me."

"Penance," she said.

He shook his head. "I told you it's more than that. You've probably forgotten this, but being with you can be nice."

"Oh, yeah, a laugh a minute."

An urge to touch her rippled through him like the ocean breeze. He wanted to pull her against him. The strength of the instinct irritated him. He shoved his hands into the pockets of his shorts.

She touched him lightly on his arm. "It means a lot that I can trust you."

Don't trust me too much, he thought, craving her. His pulse raced at her nearness and he was careful not to move a millimeter. He didn't want her to pull away. "It works both ways, Callie," he said in a low voice.

"You're so strong that I sometimes forget that you're recovering, too." She searched his face then put her arms around him.

He sucked in her closeness like a man who'd been stuck in the desert for days and she was his first drink of water. Her embrace knocked him sideways. She was sober and not crying. This was the first time she'd flat-out hugged him, and his heart and body were overwhelmed. He pulled his hands out of his pockets to put them around her, then thought better of it and returned them. He shouldn't encourage her.

On the other hand, he knew a human touch was part of healing.

Holding his breath, he slowly eased his hands out of his pockets and slid his arms around her.

She made a little sound of satisfaction and squeezed him. "This is embarrassing to admit, but I think I must be starved for hugs."

"I'm sure you can find lots of volunteers to give you hugs," he said dryly.

"Yeah, but they're not—" She broke off and pulled back slightly, looking into his eyes.

"They're not what?"

She moved her shoulders and confusion shimmered in her eyes. "I guess I don't want hugs from just anyone."

"Picky," he said, trying to lighten the conversation, even though his chest felt strange as the dickens.

She gave a lopsided smile. "Choosy. I've always thought it was a good thing to be choosy."

"Choosy's just a nice word for picky," he told her, thinking that if she decided he was going to be her hug supplier, he was in for pure torture. Heaven help him.

She began to spontaneously hug him and touch him. Every once in a while he could see it coming and brace himself for his response to her, but she often ambushed him. She clearly had no idea of her effect on him.

Brock was starting to think that the cure to his survivor guilt just might put him over the edge. She was so soft and feminine in his arms. He inhaled her scent as if it were a drug. After feeling dead for so long, she made his every cell feel alive. He spent an inordinate amount of energy trying to ignore just how alive she made him feel. He had a mission. There were steps to take, goals to be accomplished.

"You need to make some friends," he said, as they went for their run on the beach one cloudy morning.

"I probably should, but I'm not sure how. It's not really one of those things you can do through a classified ad."

"You could volunteer or join a club," he suggested.

Callie made a face and slowed to a walk. "I already told you I'm not much of a joiner."

He struggled with a ripple of frustration. "You may need to change that."

"I don't know. I don't fit in with groups real well. I didn't fit in with the military wives. They thought I was weird." She shrugged and looked at him. "And I guess I am a little weird, but isn't everyone?"

"Some are more weird than others," he said dryly.

"Oh, thanks!" She swatted him playfully. "Just the encouragement I needed to go out among the rest of humanity."

Brock laughed at her indignation then felt a few drops of rain on his shoulders. He looked up at the sky. "Oops. I think we're gonna get caught."

"And I'm not running the rest of the way back to my cottage," she said.

Glancing around, he spotted a stand of trees. "C'mon, that looks like it will be better than nothing."

The rain suddenly burst through the clouds and he

tugged her toward the trees. Water dampened her hair and face. She pulled at her T-shirt as it clung to her, then glanced at him. "This is your fault. If you hadn't dragged me out here—"

"You'd be inside moping," he finished for her.

She opened her mouth then closed it. "Maybe not. Maybe I would be working. I've been productive lately."

"Good for you."

"Probably thanks to you," she said reluctantly.

"You're welcome," he said with mock sweetness.

She stuck out her tongue at him.

Pleased to see some fire in her exchanges with him, he shook his finger at her playfully. "Don't stick out your tongue unless you plan to use it."

"How should I use it?" she asked, with a sensual curiosity in her eyes that made him regret teasing her.

"That's for you to figure out," he muttered, irritated at how quickly she made his temperature rise.

He barely saw her coming when she lifted her mouth to his mouth and kissed him quickly. She drew back, looking as surprised at her action as he was.

He stared at her in disbelief. "Why'd you do that?"

"Because you dared me to do it," she said defensively.

"I did not."

"Yes, you did," she argued, her cheeks heating. "You dared me to kiss you when you said something about using my tongue. If you didn't like it, you'll just have to get over it because you asked for it."

The combination of her indignation, embarrassment and impulsive kiss set off a chain reaction inside him of gut-clenching want. The sensations inside him were a mixture of arousal and excruciating tenderness.

Instinctively reaching for her, he pulled her against him. "I didn't ask for that kind of kiss, Callie," he told her in a voice that sounded rough to his own ears.

"What kind of kiss did you ask for?"

He lowered his mouth and showed her. He rubbed his lips over hers, relishing the shape and texture of her mouth. Gently squeezing the nape of her neck, he coaxed her lips to a more accessible position.

He had the sensation of danger as he took her mouth. It should have made him more careful, but there was too much that had been pent up inside him for too long. He slid his tongue over her lips, then inside her mouth to taste her. Surprising the hell out of him, she pressed the front of her body flush against him as if she couldn't get close enough. With each stroke of his tongue, he felt as if he were standing at the edge of a volcano ready to erupt.

She made a sound of need that affected him like an intimate touch, and went wild in his arms. Matching him caress for caress, she drew his tongue deep into her mouth the same way she would draw his hardness into her body. The knowledge made him sweat.

She squeezed his forearms with a sexy kind of desperation, then slipped her hands up under his tank top to touch his chest.

Brock felt his heart hammer in his chest. Swollen with need, he slid one of his hands down to her bottom, guiding her pelvis against the place where he ached. Feeling the tight tips of her breasts against his chest, he was filled with the need to touch her all over at once. He skimmed his hand over the edge of her breast and she turned toward him, clearly begging for more.

On fire, he wanted nothing more than to strip off her clothes and plunge inside her.

After one kiss.

She pulled away to gasp for air. "Oh, wow," she whispered.

Oh, wow was an understatement. A minuscule amount of oxygen seeped into his brain. He saw the dark arousal in her eyes, her lips were already swollen from their kiss. *He could take her now if he wanted,* the devil inside him said. *He could have Rob's woman.*

Seven

Marine Lingo Translation
Soup Sandwich: A mess. Not squared away.

He needed a beer. He needed to watch a ball game on a giant screen. He needed to get laid. Two out of three wasn't bad, he thought, as he chugged his second cold one and sat on a stool at Smiley's Bar. His Braves were having a tough time.

Hearing a chorus of feminine laughter, he glanced over his shoulder and saw the cute brunette giving him the eye again. He glanced away, thinking he could probably get something going with her if he was so inclined. He'd been walking around with a hard-on for the last two weeks. He should be inclined but, for some reason, he didn't have the stomach for anonymous sex anymore. Brock wondered if his change in attitude was due to the explosion. More than his body had been affected by it.

Sighing, he took another swig and focused on the game.

"The Braves aren't doing very well tonight, are they?" a feminine voice beside him said.

He glanced up to see the brunette who had been watching him all evening. "Yep. They can't seem to pull it together tonight. Happens to most everyone once in a while."

"I'm Candace McDonald," she said, and extended her hand. "You looked lonely over here, so I thought I would come say hello."

"Hi. I'm Brock," he said, and glanced at the screen again.

"Are you new here?" she asked, sitting next to him.

"Kinda. I'm just here for a few weeks. What about you?"

She smiled. "Darn, I should have known. All the good ones are temporary. I live here full-time and trust me, there's not much going on in the winter."

He nodded. "I can see how that would happen. It gets cold and all the visitors go away."

"And there's my job. I teach kindergarten and most of my colleagues are female. Makes it tough for a girl to meet a guy."

He looked at her again, this time from a different perspective. Maybe she could become a friend of Callie's. "You haven't been here long?"

"This is my first job out of college. I'm working this summer with an enrichment program."

"Enrichment?" he echoed.

"We do art projects and introduction to foreign languages, elementary science experiments. That sort of thing."

"Art," he said, thinking of that old saying, *if the mountain won't come to Mohammed, then Mohammed must go to the mountain.* "I know a woman, a local woman who draws art for children's books."

Her eyes widened with interest. "Really? I bet my kids would love for her to visit. You think she would be interested?"

"I think you should ask her," he said. "She's a little shy, but I bet she would say yes." He thought for a moment. "You know, you might even invite her out to lunch sometime. Here's her name and phone number," he said, and wrote down Callie's information on a paper napkin.

The young woman took the napkin and gave him a considering glance. "I wouldn't mind having lunch with you, but I get the impression you're otherwise engaged, or at least otherwise distracted." She tapped her fingernail against the napkin and lifted her eyebrow in a questioning way.

He almost denied it. He definitely wasn't engaged, however he couldn't honestly say he wasn't distracted by Callie. "Give her a call. You'll be glad you did."

"Okay," she said, taking another napkin and writing her name and phone number on it. "You give me a call if you change your mind."

"Okay," he said, accepting the napkin. But he knew he wouldn't call her.

Brock came to the conclusion that the only way he was going to be able to keep his hands off of Callie was by helping her get a life and by helping her get a man. Although part of him vehemently rebelled at the notion of Callie being with another man, he knew that was what she needed. Sure, no man would ever be able to replace Rob, but another man could hold her, kiss her and cherish her. Another man could make love to her. The very thought of it made his blood pressure spike, but he believed it was necessary for her reentry into the land of the living.

Callie was an affectionate woman and she needed someone, besides a cat, on whom to pour all her affection.

After getting a look at her wardrobe of T-shirts, jeans and sweats, he faced another hard truth—Callie needed to go shopping for clothes, and he was going to have to accompany her.

Arming himself with the *Atlanta Constitution,* he picked her up on Wednesday afternoon and drove to a shopping mall about thirty miles away. He had told her he was taking her for a drive, not out to get a new wardrobe.

When he pulled into a parking space, she looked at him in confusion. "Why are we stopping?"

"We're going shopping."

"What do you need?"

His lips twitched. "I don't need anything. You need some new clothes."

"No, I don't."

"Yes, you do. You're going to start participating in more activities than walking on the beach, feeding the cat and painting. You need a couple of dresses and some shirts that fit you instead of hanging off you."

She frowned at him. "Are you criticizing my style?"

"Yes," he said flatly, and opened the car door and got out.

"I didn't bring any money," she protested.

"That's okay. You can use my credit card. If you dent it too much, then you can pay me back." He opened her car door. "Your adventure awaits."

With narrowed eyes, she glanced at the newspaper he'd tucked under his arm. "You think you're just going to cruise through this with a newspaper while I do all the work?"

"They'll be your clothes. You should do the work," he told her.

She stood up and got in his face. "Uh-uh. You, Mr. Smarty-Pants, are going to have to shop, too. Yes, that four-letter word that men hate so much. You're going to have to make suggestions and offer opinions. If I have to suffer through this, then you do, too."

Brock quickly realized he'd unleashed a shopping she-devil. She dragged him with her to every women's clothing store. Not content to let him find a seat in the food court so he could read the sports section, she consulted him on colors and styles, hem length, pants versus dresses.

"You're an artist. You know a lot more about color and stuff like that than I do."

"Well, you must have an opinion," the shopping she-devil said. "Since you're convinced I need a new wardrobe. Lingerie is next," she said with an evil smile.

He groaned as he followed her into a shop filled with satin, silk and lace.

"What do you think of this?" she asked him, pointing to a black bra. "It's supposed to do miraculous things for your breasts without surgery. I'm so small," she complained.

"Small isn't all bad," he murmured, running his fingers over the satin cup, imagining taking the bra off of her and teasing her nipples into tight buds, wrapping his tongue around them and… His internal body temperature shot up several degrees.

"Which color do you like best?" she asked, holding up a black thong in one hand and a red thong in the other.

His throat tightened up when his mind easily produced the image of her tight little bottom in either of those scraps of satin. "Either," he said hoarsely. "Both."

"Okay. I'll go try some of these on. You're in luck," she said, scooping up another couple of bras.

"How?" he asked, unable to see any vestige of good luck for him in this situation.

"You can read your newspaper now. I'm way too shy to model this stuff for you."

He watched her leave and tried to decide if that meant he was lucky or not. He went outside the store and found a bench. Sitting down, he took out his paper and turned to the sports section. Was he really lucky because he wasn't actually seeing her in the satin bras and thongs? His mind conjured an image of Callie wearing the black thong and black satin bra, her fiery hair in disarray and her lips painted red, but smudged from his kisses.

He could feel the silk of her skin beneath his fingertips, the taste of her tongue as he took her mouth again. He loved the way her hands felt on his bare skin, the feminine wanting she expressed with every little movement she made. The way she drew his tongue into her mouth made him think about how she would draw him deep into her body.

He wanted more. He wanted to caress her nipples. He wanted to taste them until she was wet and swollen with wanting between her thighs. He wanted to touch her in her secret places and make her bloom with so much need she trembled from it.

In some corner of his perception, Brock noticed the newspaper twitching. He glanced down at his hands clenched around the edges of the paper, crumpling it. He was hard. He was sweating. Swearing under his breath, he shook his head to clear it. He hadn't even seen her try on that lingerie, but he knew he would be tormented with his own images for a long, long time.

Two days later, he knew he was going to have to be firm with her. He decided to try yet another strategy to get past his strange feelings toward Callie. He'd decided to pretend she was his sister. "It's Friday night," Brock told her, expecting protests, excuses and reasons to procrastinate. "We're going to a bar."

She wrinkled her nose. "I don't really feel like going out tonight. Besides, I'm going to have to be social in another way. I got a call from some teacher at a local elementary school today and she asked me to come and help with a special program for her kindergarten class. I can't figure out how she got my name."

Good, he thought. The woman he'd met the other night had followed up.

"We started talking and she asked me to meet her for a drink sometime. So, see, it's not necessary for me to go to a bar tonight."

"You need practice," he said. "You need practice interacting with adults."

She shot him a look of disapproval. "That's not very nice. My social skills are fine."

"I wasn't talking about your social skills. I'm talking about social experience. You need practice. Can you tell me that isn't true?"

"Well, maybe, but—"

"Face it, Callie. Most of your social experience is with Rob. You need to start getting some of your own experience."

She sighed. "I was hoping you wouldn't push for this so soon, but I had a very bad feeling about that shopping spree. Like payback was going to be hell."

"Fair is fair," he said, remembering how she had relished putting him through his paces during the shopping trip, too.

"I don't know where any bars are," she protested. "And I really need to spend some more time in the studio tonight and—"

"Excuses," he said, shaking his head. "Procrastination. Get your butt into one of those new dresses, brush your hair and put on some of that war paint I bought for you and we'll head out."

Fifteen minutes later, Callie tottered into the room on a pair of stiletto heels and wearing a blue dress that faithfully followed her every curve. She bit her lush painted lips and Brock thought of a thousand reasons *not* to take her to a bar tonight. His goal was to get Callie out among adults and find a guy or two she could spend some time with. He was trying to help her find a man to dance with, maybe kiss, maybe more…

Regret burned in his gut. He didn't want some other man pawing her. Clenching his jaw and sucking in a mind-clearing breath, he reminded himself that this wasn't about what he wanted. It was about what Callie needed.

"Good job," he said, forcing himself to use the same tone he would use when a PFC performed well.

"I shouldn't have gotten these shoes. I'm going to break my neck," she said.

"You'll be fine. I imagine there will be at least a half-dozen guys willing to catch you if you fall."

"And if there aren't?"

"Then I will," he promised, but part of him wondered who was really doing the falling.

He escorted her out the door, to his car and toward a dance bar down the beach. Glancing at her, he noticed she was clasping her hands together so tightly he wondered if she would draw blood.

"Nobody's going to bite you—unless you want them to," he told her.

She shot him a hostile look. "Thanks for the reassurance. I feel so much better."

He shrugged and turned on the radio to help calm her nerves. "Approach it from a military point of view. What's the worst case scenario?"

"Just one worst case scenario?" she asked. "I thought there were at least a dozen. I could trip over these heels and fall down in front of everyone."

"We covered that one. Several someones will help you up."

"It would still be embarrassing."

"But you would live. If it bothered you that much,

you could go to a different bar where no one had seen you fall."

"What if someone makes a move on me?" she asked in a tense voice.

"Before I answer that question, I need to know if you would want them to make a move or not."

She glared at him. "Not, of course."

"No of course about it, Callie. You're single now."

"I don't feel single."

"That's because you haven't gotten out enough."

She sighed. "You still haven't answered my question."

"If some guy makes a move on you, you can turn him down, or I can help," he said.

"Then there's the opposite end of the spectrum. What if nobody talks to me and I sit there all alone feeling like a dud?"

"Is it better to sit alone feeling like a dud at home?"

She gave an exaggerated nod. "It's much better to feel like a dud in the privacy of my home. That way, I'm just lonely, not lonely and humiliated."

Brock pulled into the gravel parking lot of the bar and rubbed his hand over his face. This could be more challenging than he'd predicted. "Tell you what, I'll buy you a drink and talk to you for a half hour, then give the other guys some room."

She frowned, but nodded. "Okay."

"Okay, scoot."

She wrinkled her brow in confusion. "What do you mean, scoot?"

"I mean go make your entrance."

"By myself?"

"Of course. If you walk in with me, everyone will assume we're together and that will defeat the purpose of this exercise."

"And just so I'm clear on this, what is the purpose of this exercise?"

"The purpose is for you to engage in conversation with adult males and females, dance if you're so inclined, and possibly make arrangements for future dates or—"

She held up her hand. "Let's just work on the conversation part first. I'm not interested in dating. I'm not sure I ever will be," she said firmly.

Brock didn't bother to correct her. No use arguing over home plate when he had to get her to first base. He cocked his head toward the bar. "Stalling time is over."

She made a face. "You, you, you better come in after me, just in case…" Her mouth hung open as if she were searching for the right words.

"Just in case you get stampeded by every male in the place," he offered for her.

She snorted in disbelief and shoved open her car door. "Yeah, right. Like that's ever going to happen to me."

Brock watched her get out of the car and walk toward the entrance to the bar, her hips swinging from side to side as she planted one high heel in front of the other. Second—and third—thoughts chugged through his mind. Maybe this hadn't been a good idea after all. Maybe she wasn't ready.

Maybe *he* wasn't ready.

Eight

Marine Lingo Translation
Crumbcatcher: Mouth.

Brock gave Callie three minutes before he strolled into the bar. Spotting her from the doorway, he was surprised to see her already chatting animatedly with a man. He sidled over to an empty table that gave him a good view but wasn't too close to the bar, and watched the two of them talk.

After a few minutes, it became clear that they were talking about a couple of paintings hanging from the walls. The man carried her drink and his beer and guided her to one of the pictures. They appeared to discuss the painting for several minutes then returned to the bar. Callie wrote something down on a napkin and handed it to the man.

Brock raised his eyebrows and took a swig of his Corona. If she'd given him her phone number, the guy must have been smooth. He studied the man carefully. He looked midthirties, a little on the short side, dressed more appropriately for the city than this beach bar where drinks were served in plastic cups, and he'd slicked back his hair with gel.

The man kept moving way too close to Callie for Brock's taste, but she didn't seem to mind. She smiled and laughed.

Brock frowned. A restless sensation skittered through him. It was all well and good to get Callie out and dating again, but she needed to develop some self-protective skills toward men. He didn't want anyone taking advantage of her.

Acting in her best interest—at least that was what he told himself—he ambled to Callie's side. She smiled at him. "Brock, I've met another artist. He did those paintings on the far wall. Aren't they fantastic?"

Brock nodded in a noncommittal way. "Yeah. Are you from around here?"

The man shook his head and extended his hand. "No. Just passing through. I have a gallery in Atlanta. I'm Rick Lowry."

"Brock Armstrong," he said.

"Brock is moving to Atlanta soon. He's an architect."

"It's a great city. I prefer Boston or New York, but I have other reasons for staying." He glanced toward the other side of the bar and his face lit up. "There's

George waving me over." He turned back to Brock and pulled a card out of his pocket. "Listen, if you need anything when you get to Atlanta, give me a call. I know the best bars." He smiled at Callie. "Keep in touch. Let me know when you want to do a show. Bye now."

Brock took a deep gulp of his beer as he felt Callie looking at him.

"I think George is his partner," Callie said.

Brock nodded. "I got that impression. I imagine he won't be asking you to dance."

"No, but he might ask you," she said and chuckled.

Brock shot her a sideways glance. "Aren't you the funny one? I send you in here to hook up with a guy and you immediately find the one who doesn't like women."

Her lips twitched. "I wouldn't say he doesn't like women at all. He just may not like them—" she waved her hand "—romantically."

At that moment, the band on the patio geared up, filling the area with loud music.

"That's not a…"

Brock leaned closer, straining to hear her. "What did you say?"

"I said that's not all bad since this is my first time out and I told you I'm not interested in—"

"Excuse me," a male voice interjected.

Callie and Brock looked up in surprise.

The man cocked his head toward the dance floor. "Wanna dance?"

Brock watched the man's gaze slide over Callie's body like a laser-guided missile, not missing a curve. He fought a sudden strange urge to cover her with something—a blanket, on oversize beach towel, his body. Taking a deep breath, he dismissed the instinct and told himself this was what he'd wanted for her. He glanced at Callie and saw her jaw hanging slightly open in surprise.

She started to shake her head and Brock intervened. "Sure she will. Callie loves to dance."

Callie blinked then glared at him. "I, uh—"

"She's just a little shy," Brock said.

"I can help with that," the guy said in a seductive voice that made Brock grind his teeth. The man extended his hand and Callie hesitantly accepted.

No big deal, he told himself. This was what he'd wanted for Callie. Besides, the band wasn't playing a slow song, so the guy wouldn't be putting his hands all over her.

Sighing, Brock ordered another beer and watched Callie. Twenty minutes later, he glanced at his watch. The guy must have been persuasive if he'd hung on to her this long. Brock heard the music slow and watched the man pull her into his arms.

His gut clenched and he held his breath. Swearing at himself, he deliberately took a breath. Why was he overreacting like this? It was just a dance. It was what he'd wanted for her.

Glued to the sight of her, he felt her gaze connect with his when the man's back was facing Brock.

Even from this distance in the darkened bar, he saw emotions churning in her eyes. He glimpsed a combination of discomfort warring with need. She bit her lip and pulled away. He could practically hear the apology. He saw it written on her face as she left the dance floor.

She sat next to him and took a sip of her now-melted margarita. "Are you happy now?"

Not exactly, he thought. "It's a step," he said. "The first one is the hardest."

"I guess," she murmured. "Can we walk out on the beach for a couple of minutes? I need some air."

"Sure," he said. "Do you want your drink?"

She shrugged, but shook her head. "No."

They walked past the band and dance floor to the back door. Callie slipped off her shoes and carried them in one hand as she stepped onto the sand. "Oh, barefoot on the sand feels so much better than these heels."

Glad he'd skipped socks, Brock ditched his loafers and joined her. They walked closer to the shore and he watched her inhale the ocean breeze. She seemed restless and edgy.

"Was it that bad? I thought you told me that you like to dance," he said.

"I do like to dance, but I didn't feel comfortable with that man."

"Probably because you didn't know him. You might have grown more comfortable."

She shrugged. "I felt a lot more comfortable with you," she said and met his gaze.

He saw flickers of hunger in her eyes that matched what he was feeling for her. His gut tightened. "Maybe you shouldn't feel quite so comfortable with me."

"Why?" she asked, cocking her head to one side.

Brock looked away and stifled a groan. How did he explain that he wanted her so much, he went to bed every night burning with it? How did he confess his carnal need for her and still have her trust him?

She put her hand on his arm and he instinctively tightened his bicep. He'd spent so much time denying himself, he hadn't realized how much her touch could effect him.

"Why?" she repeated, her gaze imploring.

Brock sighed. "Because I may be doing my damndest to look after you, but I'm still a man. It's been a long time since I've been with a woman and being around you—" He broke off. "Being with you reminds me of what I'm missing."

Her eyes widened in disbelief. "You want me?"

He felt a scratchy irritation skitter down his neck. "What's so surprising about that? You're warm and sexy. You're beautiful."

She lifted her hand to his forehead. "Are you sure you're not ill? Delusional? I'm not beautiful. And I couldn't be sexy if I tried."

"You don't have to try. You haven't been looking at yourself like I have," he muttered, covering her hand with his and lowering it to his mouth. He rubbed his mouth over her palm, then darted his tongue over the inside of her wrist. He did the seductive move as a warning. *Know the limits, he was trying to tell her. Don't push the boundaries or you might get something you don't want.*

Expecting her to gasp and jerk her hand away, he was surprised when she stared at him in fascination and allowed him to continue to hold her hand in his.

Moving closer, she licked her lips and the sight of her pink tongue made him hard. "I want you, too," she whispered. "I feel guilty about it. Like I shouldn't," she continued in a rush.

Her confession made his heart jump. "You shouldn't want me," he told her. "I'm not the right kind of guy for you."

"The right kind of guy died," she said, her voice turning bitter. "I may fight it, but I'm still breathing, still living, still hurting and now wanting. I'm tired of feeling guilty for living when Rob died."

"You shouldn't feel guilty for living, Callie," he said, cradling her jaw, fighting the urge to draw her to him.

She closed her eyes. "Sometimes I think I must have turned into the worst woman on the planet. I want you. I don't love you, but I want you. I want to kiss you and touch you. I want you to touch me and get rid of this frustration and dissatisfaction that never goes away. I want to be one of those women you've had where they know the game and don't care."

Brock's temperature climbed several degrees. It would be so easy to take advantage of her now. So easy. He could pull her against him and touch her. He could kiss away the guilt and any vestiges of resistance. "You're not that kind of woman," he told her.

"Maybe I am," she said, opening her eyes, and he could feel the heat of her arousal between them. It thrummed with a dark and desperate need that matched his. "Maybe I've changed. Maybe I'm terrible and wicked because I want you, but I'd just be using you." She inhaled audibly and pulled her hand from his. "Oh, I can't believe I'm telling you this. It's crazy. I've gone crazy," she said and turned away.

She was his for the taking. The knowledge was unbearably tempting. She could ease the burning inside him. But how could he justify taking Rob's woman?

Rob was dead, a voice inside him ruthlessly reminded him. Rob couldn't take care of Callie's needs anymore. Brock couldn't take care of her the way she needed to be cared for, but he was confident he could take care of her in bed. He could let her use him.

What a joke, he thought. As if he would be doing her a favor. He was dying to get close to her, inside her.

Swearing under his breath, he scraped his hand through his hair. Maybe he was making this too complicated. Maybe this was part of the healing process for Callie. Maybe she needed to have sex with him so she could be ready for the guy she would really fall for. The thought pinched, but he brushed the sensation aside. Maybe he was looking for a justification where there was none.

Maybe it was time to stop thinking so damn much. His heart pounding in his chest, he moved closer to her, right behind her so he could smell a hint of her soft, sweet fragrance. "Are you sure about this?" he asked in a low voice against her ear.

"Yes," she said. "How horrible am I?"

Feeling like Satan himself, he lifted her hair from the side of her neck and lowered his mouth to brush his lips over her skin, while he slid his other hand around to her belly. "Maybe we should skip the recriminations and just agree to be horrible together."

He felt her shudder in his arms, then she turned around to face him and lifted her hands to cradle his head. "I've never been with a man like you."

"So we're even. I've never been with a woman like you," he said, seeing the lack of confidence in her eyes. "Maybe you can teach me something."

She gave a short, catchy laugh of disbelief. "Fat chance."

"You can try," he said, moving his hands around to the back of her waist and pulling her against him. "C'mon, Callie," he taunted. "Give it a try." Lowering his head, he pressed his mouth against hers and rubbed from side to side, absorbing the taste and texture of her lips. The kiss was a tease to himself, to her, and as she slid her fingers through his hair and gave a soft moan, he wanted more.

Opening his mouth, he drew her lips into his, tasting her, wanting to inhale her sweetness. She responded by sliding her tongue against his in a shy, but sensual shimmy that did crazy things to his nerve endings. Another moan escaped her lips and he felt the fire in his belly burn higher.

He opened his mouth and consumed her lips and tongue with his. As if there was a raging inferno pushing him onward, he rocked against the cradle of her femininity. The friction made him even harder. She ground against him in response, sucking his tongue deep into her sweet recesses.

She was so warm, so sexy, so ready. He felt the fringe of her desperation ripple through him. She caught him off guard when she tugged his shirt free from his jeans. Her hands on his belly were a welcome surprise.

He slid his hands lower to cup her sweet bottom as they moved against each other. He grew harder with each movement, each stolen breath she took. Unable to resist the temptation of her bare skin, he slipped one of his hands up under the hem of her dress, higher, finding her naked derriere. She was wearing the damn thong.

He broke into a sweat. The image of her naked bottom jerked him into third gear. He slid his fingers over the silky rounded contours. She undulated against him, as hot and bothered as he was. He could ditch this little scrap of silk and slide inside her right now. She wasn't at all cognizant of their proximity to the public bar, and he barely was.

He should stop, show some sanity, but oh—she felt so good, and she was wiggling against him like she couldn't get close enough. He wanted just a little more. *Just a little more,* he thought, as he slid his fingers between her legs and found her warm and wet.

"Oh, you feel so good," he muttered.

She moaned into his mouth and he stroked her, finding her bead of femininity swollen. He rubbed her with his thumb and plunged his finger inside her. The pitch of her voice changed, higher, more desperate. More than anything, he wanted to take care of the need he felt and heard coming from inside her.

He French-kissed her as he stroked her sweet spot and she opened her mouth gasping. He felt her contract intimately in his hand. "I—I—ohhhhhh." He covered her mouth with his to conceal the volume, drinking in her cry of pleasure.

"Oh my G—" She broke off and gasped for air, clinging to him. She ducked her head in his shoulder. "I don't know whether to die from embarrassment or just thank you," she finally managed in a husky breath.

"Why embarrassment?" he asked, trying unsuccessfully to nudge her head upward. "Embarrassment," he muttered, still hard as a brick. "Do you have any idea how sexy you were?"

"Yeah, right," she said in disbelief. "Sexy like a cat in heat. Screaming and mewing. Did I leave claw marks?"

"No," he said and chuckled. "But the evening's young."

She slowly lifted her head, her eyes full of pleasure and shimmering with the beginning of desire.

"I've never done that—" she cleared her throat self-consciously "—on the—"

"Beach. There's a drink called Sex on the Beach. I take it you've never had it."

She shook her head. "I never had body slammers, either."

"Looks like I'm leading you down the road to perdition. Are you sure you wanna go?"

Her eyes darkened. "Race ya," she said. "Can we go to your place?"

Nine

Marine Lingo Translation
Mattress pressing: Sleeping.

Brock drove them to his condo. Callie didn't say a word, but he could practically hear her emotions rattling inside her with the force of a hurricane.

He was still aroused, raring to go, ready in every way. He took a deep breath and worked at putting out the fire, or at least bringing it under control.

She'd lost her nerve. He felt a sinking disappointment, and something deeper, and shook it off. Maybe it was for the best.

He pulled into a spot in front of his condo and shifted into a Park. Sighing, he turned to her. "Hey, I can take you home. It's no problem."

"Why?" she asked.

Confused by the note of surprise in her voice, he looked at her. "You haven't said anything. You're having second thoughts. I understand."

"I'm not having second thoughts," she said.

Growing impatient, he rolled his eyes. "Callie, you've been completely silent."

"Well, excuse me, but maybe I'm a little nervous. It's been a while for me. And you're, well, you're different," she said in a huffy voice. "What if you end up thinking I'm a dud in bed and—"

He couldn't hold back a chuckle.

"And now you're laughing at me. Maybe I *am* having second thoughts," she said, crossing her arms over her chest.

Laughing again in some crazy combination of relief and frustration, he pulled her against him. "Don't worry about being a dud."

"Easy for you to say, Mr. Romeo."

He pressed his forehead against hers. "I told you I'm no Romeo. I didn't have to work that hard. Romeo had to try harder."

"That's right. The women fall into your hands like water from the faucet. I'm just like the rest of them, Brock."

"No you're not," he said. "No—"

She lifted her finger to his lips to stop his words. "I'm just like the rest of them. I need to be just like the rest of them."

She wasn't, but he wasn't going to argue with her about it. Not right now, anyway. This was one freakin' weird situation, but Brock had the odd feeling that he needed to let Callie see what a woman she was—in every sense of the word.

He kissed her and her response was warm and inviting. His banked arousal flared again. "Let's go inside," he murmured.

He led her inside and into the den. "Can I get you something to drink?"

"That would be nice," she said.

He pulled out a bottle of white wine he'd bought a week ago and poured two glasses. The wine wasn't going to do a damn thing to dampen his libido. He figured he would need to be run over by a truck in order to lose this edgy gotta-have-her feeling. Maybe not even then.

He found her on his balcony, enjoying the ocean breeze, and offered her a glass of wine.

"You have a great view," she said, accepting the glass and taking a long sip.

"I do," he said, looking at her.

She caught his gaze and smiled, shaking her head. "I meant the ocean."

"It's okay. I like what I'm looking at better."

"You're a flatterer," she chided, taking another sip.

"Not me. Just call 'em like I see 'em." He stepped closer to her, inhaling her scent as he slid his arm around the front of her and drew her against him.

"Hmm. You're warm," she murmured.

"You cold?"

"Not really. But your warmth feels good."

He planned to make her feel a helluva lot more than *good*.

"Have you ever made love on a balcony?" she asked.

Surprised by her question, he grinned in the darkness. "No. Why?"

"Just curious. I imagine you've had sex in more interesting places than I have."

Setting down his glass of wine, he turned her to face him. "Do you wanna make love on the balcony?"

"Maybe," she said a little defensively. "What if I do?"

He felt his grin grow. "Then we'll make love on the balcony."

She bit her lip. "Or maybe I'd like to sometime."

Bold, then timid. She was going to kill him. *Ah, but what a way to go.* Backing against the wall, he pulled her with him. "I'll make a note to check the security of the railing," he said, lowering his mouth and French-kissing her. She tasted of wine and sweetness.

He pulled the wineglass from her hand and put it on the small wrought-iron table beside them. Her lips and tongue chased his, and with every little stroke of her tongue, he grew hotter and harder.

He ran his hands down her back to her bottom. "You feel so good," he muttered.

"You do, too," she said, her body flush with his.

He continued to dally with her lips, driving himself a little more crazy. He could feel her warming up, growing hotter and more restless. Her fingers squeezed his biceps then slid up to his shoulders. She rubbed against him and he could feel the hard tips of her breasts even through her clothing. He wanted to rip off those clothes and plunge inside her.

Slow, he coached himself. It's been a while for her. It'll be better if it's slow.

She made a sound of frustration and tugged at the buttons of his shirt. He heard the sound of one clicking on the concrete floor as it fell.

"Sorry," she murmured.

"No problem," he managed in a voice that sounded hoarse to his own ears.

"I like your chest," she whispered, her hands floating over his bare skin like a breeze. She buried her face in his chest then slid her tongue over his throat. "I like the way you taste."

Brock swallowed an oath at the surge of arousal that pumped through him. He was supposed to be the experienced one, the one in control.

She tugged her straps down and pressed her small, bare breasts against his chest and sighed as if in relief. "Sorry, I just needed to feel you."

"No apologies necessary," he said, thinking she was hotter than a firecracker and he wanted all her heat and fire. He lifted his hands and slid his fingers between them to touch the hard tips of her breasts.

She moaned against his throat. *Sensitive,* he thought, a rush of delight running through him. He played with her nipples and kissed her until her gasps made him sweat. Blindly, he groped for a chair and sank down onto it, pulling her onto his lap.

He sucked her hard nipple into his mouth and she made a sexy, keening sound of pleasure. She pressed her breast against him and he gently nipped the tip and laved it with his tongue.

Each sound she made was like another intimate stroke. He slid one of his hands between her legs and found her wet and warm. "I want to be inside you, Callie. As deep as I can get."

Shuddering, she gave him an openmouthed kiss that made him feel as if he were going to explode. Pushed to the edge of his restraint, he stood and carried her to his bedroom. He put her down on his bed and shucked his jeans, then reached to his bedside table for the condoms he'd bought last week. He tore one open and put it on, then followed her down onto the bed.

He wanted to plunge inside her this second, but he wanted to make sure she was ready for him. He found her swollen nubbin of femininity and rubbed it with his thumb. She arched against him.

"Brock."

She said his name in a hot, restless, needy whisper that felt like a drug flowing through his veins. He wanted to consume every inch of her. He stripped off her thong and buried his face between her legs, kissing her intimately, licking and sucking her hot spot.

He felt her come apart, and her climax was the biggest turn-on he'd ever experienced. Rising, he spread her legs farther apart and plunged inside her.

He distantly heard her barely audible sound of relief mingle with his. She paused a moment, her eyes widening as if his size was more than she'd expected.

Then she undulated beneath him.

Brock swore at the tight sensation. Her hair scattered over his bedspread like wild red-gold ribbons, her mouth swollen from his kisses, her eyes dark with arousal, her small breasts and tight nipples all a picture of the darkest, most forbidden fantasy he'd conjured.

She moved again in invitation.

"Take me," she said.

And he did, plunging into a rhythm that stretched and caressed. When she wrapped her legs around his waist, he felt something inside him tear at the sexy display of trust, and his orgasm ripped through him like buckshot.

Several moments passed before he could breathe or think. His heart still pounding as if he'd run a race, he rolled onto his back beside Callie. He swore.

"Is that bad or good?" she asked.

He took her hand and laced his fingers through hers. "Great. Amazing."

"Do you think it was so intense because it's been so long for both of us?"

"It could have been part of it," he said, but he knew that wasn't all. The dark, driving need he felt for her wasn't just because he'd been abstinent for a long while. He turned onto his side and looked at her. "There's one way to find out."

She looked up at him and smiled. "Really? You could do it again tonight?"

Her question made him wonder what her love life with Rob had been like, but he didn't want to go near the subject—not with his mind, certainly not with their conversation.

"Yeah, we can go again. If you want…" He lifted her hand to his mouth and kissed it.

She slid her hand over his jaw and the combination of how sexy she looked and how sweetly she touched him undid something inside him. "I think I want," she said and urged his mouth down to hers.

Hours later, after they'd made love more times than he'd thought possible, he looked up to find her sitting at the bottom of his bed with her arms holding her knees close to her chest. He suddenly felt a distance between them and a painful sensation tightened his gut. Regret. She regretted being with him. He could practically taste it.

"I think I should go home now."

He wanted to ask why, but he wasn't sure he wanted the answer, so he didn't. "Okay. Let me pull on my clothes."

He got dressed and she did the same, her eyes never meeting his as she stepped into her thong and zipped her dress. She ran her fingers through her tangled hair and winced.

"You want a brush?"

"No, I'll just wait until I get home."

They'd been as close as a man and woman could get, yet she wouldn't look at him. He felt oddly snubbed, irritated.

They walked to his car and he noticed how careful she was not to brush up against him. That irritated him more. He started the engine and drove the short distance to her cottage. He cut the engine and they sat in silence for a full moment.

"Thank you for bringing me home," she said in a small, stilted voice.

Brock clenched his jaw. An hour ago, she'd been crying out his name, begging him to come inside her. "No problem. I'm at your service."

She must have heard the slight edge to his voice. She looked at him. "I've never had an affair. I'm not exactly sure how to do this. What do I do now?"

He relaxed a millimeter. "What do you want to do?"

"I don't know. I feel weird."

He nodded, thinking in all the times he'd been intimate with a woman, the evening had never ended like this. But then, he'd never been with Callie before.

He leaned closer to her and lowered his head, brushing a kiss to her forehead. "Don't try to figure it all out tonight."

"It would give me a headache."

He chuckled. "I'm flattered."

She looked at him blankly then her eyes widened. "Oh, I'm probably supposed to tell you that you were great in bed, aren't I?"

He lifted his hand. "No, not necessary at all. It's

just if you're gonna get the headache complaints, they're usually before."

"Well you were very good." She looked away then back at him as if something was troubling her. "Maybe too good. Thank you for the evening. G'night," she said and slipped out of the car.

As he watched her walk into her house, he wanted to go after her and ask her what she'd meant by *too good. How could a man be too good in bed?* She hadn't said it in a complimentary way.

Brock frowned and started the car, jerking it into gear. By the time he arrived back at his condo, every other word flying through his mind was an oath. What a kooky, weird woman. *Too good, my ass,* he thought. She hadn't been exactly shabby herself.

Stomping into his house, he headed for the refrigerator and poured himself a glass of wine. He swore again. After the amount of sex he'd had tonight, he should be dead on his feet, ready for a coma. Instead, he was irritated, wondering what her problem was. He knew she'd wanted him, she'd matched his eagerness. He hadn't misread her.

Scowling, he paced the den. He collected their abandoned glasses from the balcony and tried not to focus on how she had felt in his arms, how she had tasted. Pulling the patio door shut, he turned on the television to a late-night infomercial. He needed to fill up his brain with something besides Callie.

Taking a gulp of his wine, he paced from one end of the den to the other. He paced to the bedroom and came to a stop. The bed mocked him. He smelled her scent and she was there—her hair splayed out on his bedcover, her legs tangled with his, her voice urging him on.

Damn her. He stripped the bed and put on fresh sheets, but before he tossed the sheets into the washer, he couldn't resist inhaling another draft of her. She had told him she wanted to be just like all the other women he had known. He'd never had any problem putting a woman behind him.

He'd better not start now with her.

The next morning, after another restless night, he grimly refocused and reminded himself that he was trying to help Callie recover from her grief. It was her prerogative to act strangely. He needed, however, to keep her on track. Last night had been about healing and want.

It sure as hell hadn't been pity sex, his brain screamed at him with the same lack of pity he would expect from a drill instructor. He had relished every minute of it and would have gone back for more if…

He swore. He needed to stop thinking about it. After taking an early morning run, he waited awhile and decided to get Callie moving. One of the keys to getting her out of a rut was keeping her moving, even if that meant a run on the beach.

He pounded on the door and waited. Several moments later, she appeared at the door in a robe, her hand shielding her eyes from the sun.

"Why are you here now?"

"Time for your run." He pointed at his watch. "I gave you an extra hour."

She groaned, covering her face. "I don't feel like running today." She held the door open for a half-second then turned back into the house.

Brock caught the screen door just before it slammed shut and followed her inside. "You'll feel better once you get moving."

"No, I won't. I drank some of that nasty tequila you left here."

He lifted his eyebrows in surprise. "Why?"

"So I wouldn't think and so I would sleep. My head feels like someone is slamming it with a hammer."

"How much did you drink?"

"Just two shots, but I think it combined with the margarita and the glass of wine and—" she glanced at him then looked away "—and the activity to be too much."

"I'll get you some aspirin," he said, heading for her medicine cabinet. In some sick way, it comforted him that she'd had problems sleeping, too. After he collected the medicine, he stopped by the kitchen to fill a glass with water and grab a few crackers.

"Crackers first," he said as he stood in front of her.

She sighed. "Do you have to be so nice when I'm feeling so cranky?"

His lips twitched. She reminded him of a child that had been woken too early from her nap. "You can walk a little when the meds kick in."

She shook her head. "No, I can't."

"Why not?"

"Because my head isn't the only thing that's hurting," she said bluntly.

It took a moment for her meaning to sink in. "Oh, muscles or—"

"Try everything. Everything that hasn't been exercised that way in a long time, or maybe everything that's never been exercised that way. And I know they're necessary, but I think the condoms made it worse."

He gaped at her.

"So when we do this again, I prefer it barefoot."

He blinked, his stomach taking an odd dip. "From the way you acted last night, I didn't get the impression you wanted to do it again."

She sipped her water and pushed her hair from her face. Slowly, she met his gaze and he saw the stark emotion stamped across her fine features.

Guilt. She felt guilty as hell.

He felt it like a kick in the gut. "You really don't have—"

She shook her head and bit her lip. "I don't have it all figured out, but the thing that bothered me most was that I liked it better with you than I remember liking it with Rob."

Ten

Marine Lingo Translation
Cool beans: Everything is fine.

She could have knocked him over with her pinkie finger. Brock stared at her. No, make that her pinkie fingernail.

Her eyebrows furrowed. "I don't really want to talk about it. It feels disrespectful or dishonorable or scuzzy."

"Okay," he said, not eager to hear the intimate details of Callie's sexual experiences with Rob.

"But it just always seemed to go too fast and just when I started to get into it," she said with a shrug, "it would be over."

Speechless, Brock nodded. "I understand if you don't want to talk about it."

"I really appreciate it, but it's a sensitive subject. It always was. Rob never really wanted to talk about it and I just figured something might be wrong with me."

"Trust me, Callie, there's nothing wrong with you. Nothing at all," he said, remembering how hot she'd been in his arms last night.

"Are you sure?" she whispered.

Her uncertainty ripped at something inside him. The fragility of the moment required a careful response. He sank onto the sofa beside her. "I'm pretty sure," he said, "but there's only one real way to be sure. We'd have to do it again."

She punched his arm and laughed. "Not today. I'm too sore."

The telephone rang and she glanced toward the kitchen. "I wonder who that is," she said, rising. "Back in a minute."

He heard her pick up the phone. "Oh, Mama Newton, how are you?"

His ears perked up at the mention of Rob's last name.

"They've built a memorial in front of the library in honor of Rob?" Callie said, her voice tightening. "That's wonderful."

"You want me to come to the dedication ceremony?" he heard her ask, her voice tightening even more. Funny how his gut tightened each time he heard the tension rise in her voice.

"Of course I'll come," she said and paused. "Mama Newton, you're sweet to offer, but we've been through this before. I can't come live with you. My messy art would drive you crazy."

The conversation continued for several more minutes with a few muted responses from Callie. He heard her hang up the phone. A long moment passed before she returned to the den with her face and spirit matching the muted tone of her voice.

"Your mother-in-law?" he prompted.

She nodded, looking as tense as an overdrawn bow with her arms crossed over her chest. "Problem?"

"No," she said in a clipped, small voice. "She's a lovely person and she's always been very kind and generous to me."

"I hear a but," he said, standing, concerned at the shift in her mood.

"No buts," she insisted.

"Callie," he said, putting his hand on her shoulder. "You're acting like an overwound jack-in-the-box."

She sighed. "It's hard to hear her pain. She still can't believe he's gone and I think one of the ways she tries to keep him alive is by talking with me about him." She pushed her hair behind her ear. "I don't want to be unkind, but I always feel so sad after I talk with her." Her voice broke and she audibly swallowed. "Sometimes I think she wants me to live the rest of my life in Rob's memory. Live with her, stop drawing, stop laughing, stop—"

"Breathing," he finished for her.

She met his gaze with desperation in her eyes. "I feel bad talking about her this way."

"You wouldn't go live with her, would you?" he asked, his instincts telling him that would be one of the worst things Callie could do.

She shook her head. "I thought about it, but I took the coward's way out," she said with a short laugh. "I ran away and moved to the beach instead."

"Good choice," he said.

She shrugged her shoulders and gave him a lop-sided smile that had the ability to move past skin, bone and muscle to his heart. "We'll see. I've been drawing more lately. This kind of thing usually slows me down, though."

"Okay. What club do you want to join so you don't slow down?" he asked.

Callie wrinkled her nose. "I think I'm going to go to a meeting of the sand castle builders' club. Wanna come?"

He nodded, unable to swallow his grin. "Yeah, just remember I'm an architect, so I'm opinionated about construction."

They spent the next three hours constructing an elaborate castle made of sand. Brock had argued for something more modern, but Callie insisted on turrets and moats. Soon enough, a group of children asked if they could help and the castle became a community project.

Brock enjoyed watching Callie's interaction with the children and he became more determined than ever to nudge her to get regularly involved. She exclaimed over their diligence and creativity.

"Photographs," she said. "I've got to have photographs. Wait here while I get my cameras," she said, and ran to the cottage.

She returned with two cameras. "Okay, crowd around the back of the castle. You, too, Brock!"

He shook his head. "No. You should be in this."

She shook her head. "No, you designed it so—"

"Your nose is burned," he said, lightly touching her pink nose. "I told you that you should have put on more sunscreen."

"I'll take it," a woman said, stepping forward. "That way, both you and your husband can be in the picture."

Out of the corner of his eye, Brock saw Callie open her mouth at the same time he opened his. "Thanks," he said, beating her to the punch and tugging Callie toward the castle. "We'd appreciate that."

"You shouldn't have let her think we were—"

"The ocean would have washed away the castle by the time we explained our relationship to her," he muttered. "Just let the woman take the picture."

The passerby took several photos with each camera.

"That one's digital," Callie said. "For immediate gratification."

"Is that what you want?" Brock asked in a low voice. "Immediate gratification."

She gave a cheesy smile for the camera then turned to him with fire in her eyes. "You have a wicked mind."

"You didn't answer my question," he said.

"I like it slow."

Brock made a note of it.

* * *

Brock still wasn't happy with Callie's lack of involvement and in the back of his mind, the clock was ticking. He would be leaving for his job in Atlanta in a couple of weeks. Although it wasn't his first choice, he took Callie to visit a senior citizens' center.

"I don't like public speaking," she told him as he escorted her inside the small brick building.

"Just talk a few minutes," he told her. "The director told me the main thing these people will enjoy will be some personal interaction with you."

Sighing, she shook her head. "Do you ever think you're taking this grief treatment service to the extreme? Shopping, sex, trips to the senior citizens' center."

His mind tripped on the middle item on her list. "We only had sex one time."

"It was one night," she corrected. "But it was definitely more than one time. That's why we haven't had it again."

He'd wondered. He'd told himself she was teasing him about having sex again with him, but he spent a lot of time looking for any sign of invitation from her. None so far.

The director met them and led them to a sunny room. She introduced Callie to the surprisingly large group of people. Callie spoke for a few minutes and showed the group examples of her work. Afterward, she invited the group to experiment with the easels and pads of paper available throughout the room.

Brock watched her talk with nearly every person in the room. Her patience and the way she focused her attention on each individual impressed him. He tried to think of one woman he'd dated who would have spent more than five minutes at a senior citizens' center. None came to mind.

The men flirted with her. The women mothered her. Two hours later, he finally drove out of the parking lot.

Callie leaned her head against the headrest and sighed. "That was more fun than I expected."

"You were great," he told her.

She glanced at him. "I didn't really do much. They mostly wanted to talk."

"You paid attention. You laughed at corny jokes and acted like you were interested when you were looking at photographs of grandchildren and great-grandchildren."

"I wasn't acting. It's fun to hear people talk about things or people they're enthusiastic about."

"So maybe you're not the superintrovert you profess to be," he said.

"Do you have to rub this in?"

"I'm not gonna be here forever and I don't want you crawling back into your cave when I leave."

She turned quiet. "I keep forgetting you're going to be leaving soon."

"Are you afraid you're going to miss me?"

He felt her glance at him thoughtfully. "Well, I

think you're one of those people you get used to having around."

The note of tenderness in her voice made a knot form in his chest. He didn't know if it was longing or something else.

"Sort of like a pet allergy."

He tossed her a sideways glance.

"Or a reaction to poison ivy," she said cheerfully.

"You little witch."

"Well, if you're going to get all sloppy and sentimental about me missing you."

"I didn't get sloppy and sentimental."

"Brock, you're moving just over the state line. I can hunt you down if I want."

She wouldn't want to hunt him down, though, he knew. "You don't like Atlanta."

"That's right. So you're probably safe."

"Unless you quit being such a chicken and show some of your work besides your illustrations for the children's books."

"You're starting to remind me of a pet allergy again."

He gave a dry grin. "It's my mission in life. How am I doing?"

"Great. I'm starved."

"Would you like to go to dinner?"

"That would be nice."

"To a real restaurant in public. Two public outings in one day. Are you sure you're up to it?"

She shot him a level gaze. "I've turned a corner."

"But you're not all the way onto the new road."

"Nag, nag, nag," she said.

"Is this okay?" he asked, pointing to a seafood restaurant.

She nodded. "Looks good to me."

She ordered a Hurricane. He ordered a beer. While they waited, she doodled on a napkin. He wanted to know what she was drawing, but she snatched it away before he could see. They split an appetizer of coconut shrimp. She ordered a second Hurricane and he raised his cycbrows. "You going for another headache?"

"No," she said, and muttered something under her breath. When the waitress returned with her drink, Callie pulled the cherry from her glass and offered it to him. "You told me you liked cherries?"

He choked on the beer he'd just swallowed. He couldn't read her expression, but the way she dangled the cherry from the stem made him think about forbidden fruit. Hers in particular. He grew warmer. "Yeah," he said and popped the plump cherry into his mouth.

"Just curious," she said, stirring her drink with the straw. "When was the last time you were tested for sexually transmitted diseases?"

He dipped his head in disbelief. "Excuse me?"

"When was the last time you were—"

His heart stuttered in his chest. He waved his hand for her to stop. "They tested me for everything when I was in the hospital. Why do you ask?"

She paused for a long moment, still stirring her

drink, then met his gaze. "Because I'm not sore anymore."

Brock felt his libido jump the equivalent from one to two-hundred-and-fifty miles per hour. "Is that why you've been drinking Hurricanes?"

"It would be more gallant of you not to point that out," she said, taking a sip.

He grabbed her hand and held it in his. "You want me to be gallant?"

She bit her lip. "Not really."

He leaned toward her. "Callie, it's okay to ask for what you want."

"I guess I'm not used to feeling free to ask."

"What would you like?"

Taking a little breath as if she were shoring up her nerve, she smiled. "I would like you to please take care of the check while I go to the powder room, and then I would like to go back to your place, if that's okay with you."

Her combination of shyness and boldness did dangerous things to his heart. "Okay," he said, and signaled for the waitress while Callie left the table.

When they arrived at his condo, the sun was just beginning to set and they sat in the car to watch it. "Look how pretty the sky is," she said. "Hot pink, coral and gray-blue."

"Ever get the itch to do landscapes and water-colors?"

"Every once in a while. I often joked with Rob that I needed to go to the Caribbean so I could be inspired by the sunset, but we never went." She cleared her throat and shrugged. "It didn't really matter. My strength is drawing people. I like showing emotion in facial expressions, posture, even what they wear. And with kids, I don't have to be too subtle. It's fun." She looked at him. "What about you? Did you ever want to do a different kind of architecture?"

He nodded. "Skyscrapers, like everyone else."

"Do you ever sneak and draw a building on a napkin when you're supposed to be doing something else?" she asked.

"I used to," he said, her question reminding him of times in his life that hadn't been so driven, so serious. "I haven't had a chance in a while."

"Did you when you were in the hospital?"

"A few times," he admitted and narrowed his eyes at her. "How did you know?" he teased. "Were you watching me?"

"Well, architecture is a kind of art, so I figured you had to be a doodler at some time in your life." She met his gaze, and her eyes held a combination of fragility and resolve. "I've started doodling again," she told him.

"In the restaurant," he said with a nod. "What were you drawing?"

She hesitated. "Come on," he coaxed.

"I did it quickly, so don't expect too much." She fished the napkin out of her purse and showed it to him.

Brock stared at the portrait she'd drawn of him. It had a slight cartoon quality. His chin and cheekbones were exaggerated, but she had softened his scowl with a glint in his eye. His shoulders were overly broad and she'd emphasized his pecs. "You made me look like a superhero."

"How?" she asked, frowning as she turned the napkin around to study it.

"My shoulders aren't that broad," he said.

"Yes, they are."

"You exaggerated my pecs," he said.

"Did not," she protested. "You've got a killer body and you know it."

He knew he was in shape, but it was damn nice hearing her compliment because he knew it wasn't idle flattery. After all, this same woman had compared him to the itch associated with poison ivy. "Are you trying to seduce me?"

"With this drawing?" she asked in disbelief, then chortled with glee. "Are you that easy?"

"Depends on the woman," he said, meeting her gaze and holding it. The temperature in the car went up several degrees. He saw the wanting in her eyes. "Ask for what you want," he told her.

"Kiss me," she told him, lifting her lips to his.

He took her mouth and kissed her, searching for answers to the questions she aroused in him. How did she manage to make him feel lighter just by smiling? How did she know just what to ask him that reminded him of a more carefree time in his life? How did she make him crave being with her? Even when she was sad. She was so real. Sometimes he felt as if he'd never held a real woman until her. He flicked his tongue over hers and she responded immediately, tasting him, licking his lips as if she craved him the same way he craved her.

It wasn't possible, he told himself, but it sure felt good.

"I've never done it in a car," she murmured against his lips.

"Are you saying you want to?" he asked, pulling back slightly.

Her cheeks lit with color. "Maybe sometime."

"Not tonight?" he clarified.

"Not tonight. Can we go up to your condo now?"

"Oh, yeah," he said, his body temperature climbing at the expression in her eyes.

She slid her hand into his and walked with him up the steps. He liked the way her small hand felt in his. He liked the way she felt beside him. He felt the hum of anticipation between them.

Brock was getting the impression that Callie hadn't been encouraged to be adventurous in bed, but she was eager to experiment.

He might go to hell for it, but she could experiment on him all she wanted.

Eleven

Marine Lingo Translation
Pucker Factor: The degree of stress in a given situation.

As soon as Brock got Callie inside his condo door, he pushed her against the wall and French-kissed her until they could barely breathe.

Her lids heavy with arousal, she sighed. "Oh, wow. I'm starting to understand why you don't have trouble getting women to do what you want," she murmured.

Her comment flattered him at the same time it bothered him. He pushed the bothered part aside and sank his hands into her hair and kissed her again. It was easy to forget everything when he kissed Callie. Her taste, her scent, her response, filled him up. He slid his knee between her legs and she wriggled against him.

She made him want everything at once. He wanted to kiss her everywhere, take her every way, all at once. Frustration and desire he'd never before experienced rolled through him.

"Oh." She moaned against his throat, and he felt her tempting little cat tongue slide over his skin.

"What do you want, baby?" he asked, wanting to give her everything.

"I can barely think straight. How can I tell—" She broke off when he ground her against his swollen hardness.

"I want you to tell me what you want."

"You're doing pretty good without me telling you what to do."

He took a mind-clearing breath. "I mean it. I want you to tell me what you want. I have this feeling you haven't always gotten what you wanted or needed, and I'm going to make sure that changes. Especially tonight."

She looked up at him uncertainly. "Anything? I can ask for anything?"

"Anything," he said, but he was determined she would want him inside her before the night was over.

"Okay." She licked her lips then closed her eyes. "Looking at you is distracting. I want music. I want one glass of wine for us to share. I want the lights down low."

"Have a seat while I get the wine," he said, and handed her the remote control to the stereo system.

He heard her flick through several radio stations until she landed on jazz.

Brock's fingers fumbled as he opened the bottle of white wine he'd bought after he and Callie had made love the first time. He had thought it might happen again and he'd been in a state of anticipatory lust.

He wanted this to be so right for her. His gut tied in knots, he shook his head at himself. He couldn't remember the last time he'd been nervous with a woman. He'd always taken his signals from the woman and acted on instinct, but for some reason, with Callie, it was different. He wanted to be everything she wanted and needed.

He swore under his breath as he spilled some of the wine. He was thinking way too deeply about this. Returning the wine bottle to the fridge, he walked into the den where the lights were low and found Callie in a large overstuffed chair.

"Here it is," he said, extending the wineglass to her.

"Thanks," she said and scooted over. "Join me."

"Sure." It took some rearranging, but soon she was sitting on his lap and they were taking turns sipping the wine.

He teased her with slow, mind-drugging kisses that left him hard and her limp. She accidentally spilled some wine on his shirt.

"Oh, I'm sorry. I didn't mean to—"

"No problem," he said, pulling off his shirt and tossing it aside.

Shaking her head, she skimmed one of her hands over his chest, sending a shiver down his spine. "You are incredibly built."

"A lot of scars," he muttered. He generally ignored them, but sometimes when he stepped out of the shower, the marks on his body still caught him off guard.

"They don't bother me," she whispered, and darted her pink tongue over a jagged scar on his chest.

Every muscle inside him tightened at the soft, sensual stroke.

She paused, glancing up at him. "Hurt?"

He shook his head. "Not at all."

Her lips curved in a slow, sexy smile and she lowered her mouth to his chest again. She dropped open-mouthed kisses over his chest and torso. With each millimeter lower that she traveled, he felt himself grow harder. When she dipped her mouth just above his navel, all he could think about was her wrapping her busy tongue around him, and exploding.

That would last a whopping three seconds and she wouldn't get a thing from it. Sighing, he drew her back up to his mouth.

"You didn't like the direction I was going?"

"Too much," he said, and slid his hands under her blouse while he kissed her. He found her nipples, tight little buds already, and fondled them until she was squirming in his lap.

As if she couldn't stand the teasing sensation, she pulled off her shirt and bra and tossed them aside.

She immediately pressed her breasts against him and sighed in pleasure.

Determined to make the rest of their clothes evaporate, Brock unfastened her jeans. Following his lead, he felt her tug at the button and zipper for his jeans, too. Her fumbling only made him harder.

With a growl of frustration, she pulled away from him and ditched her own jeans then tugged at his. That primitive growl sent thunder through his pulse, and after he got rid of his jeans, he pulled her back onto his lap and drew one of her breasts into his mouth.

"Oh, wow." She moaned. "They're so small, but you make them feel so good."

"They're not too small. Just right," he said, nibbling gently on her nipple.

She moaned again and squirmed. He could feel her moistness brush against him. It would be so easy to pull her over him and slide inside. The very thought of it made him feel like he would explode.

Pushing away from him, she stood naked in front of him, tugging at his hand to join her.

"What?" he asked, fascinated by the sight of her, bare and pale with her fiery red-gold hair mussed and hanging down to her shoulders.

"Dance with me," she coaxed. "Dance naked with me."

The invitation was so sexy it almost hurt to accept. As soon as he took her hand in his, she pressed herself flush against him and urged his mouth to hers.

Brock couldn't think of anything more erotic than having Callie kiss him while her silky legs slid against his and her bare belly brushed him intimately. She stretched on tiptoe, inviting him to slide against her where she was wet and swollen.

Brock accepted the invitation. She felt like warm honey on him. He wanted so badly to plunge inside… He swore.

"I need to get a condom," he muttered, loath to move away from her.

"No, you don't," she said, brushing her lips over his in a teasing caress.

"What do you mean?"

"I mean I got something from the doctor so we don't have to use anything else."

"The pill?"

She shook her head and made a little sound of frustration. "No. I took care of it. No worries. No babies."

For an instant, the image of Callie, big and pregnant with his baby, flashed through his mind. His heart squeezed tight in a strange way. Alarm shot through him. *Where the hell had that thought come—*

She brushed against him again, distracting him.

She was a delectable, wiggling, irresistible combination and she was so hot he could barely stand it. He could feel her heat, her want, and it drove his excitement level straight through the roof.

"Oh, babe, you're making it hard for me to take my time," he said, both tortured and stimulated as she rocked against him. "What do you want, Callie?"

Her shiver of anticipation sent his libido up another notch. "I like it all," she murmured, rubbing her mouth over his chest. "I like the way you touch me, the way you kiss me. I like it all."

The dark sensual expression in her eyes tore his already shredded restraint. He pushed her back against the chair they'd shared and kissed his way down her silky, smooth skin. Her flat belly rippled as he tasted her belly button and when he went lower, she gasped. He tasted her intimately, rubbing his tongue over her swollen bead.

She arched against his mouth and her breath came in sexy little gasps that made him crazy with need. She said his name over and over again as he felt her climax against him.

"Brock, pleeeeeeease."

"Please what?" he asked, his body bucking with the need to be inside her.

She slid her hands over his hips and pulled him between her legs. "I want you so bad."

"How, Callie?" he asked at the edge of his control. He felt his muscles bunch and coil with the effort to restrain himself.

"In me," she said, arching her hips upward in a glorious feminine invitation that he would have to be dead not to accept.

Unable to hold back any longer, he plunged inside her. He heard her moan mingle with his at the delicious sensation. She was wet, tight and irresistible. He pumped inside her, groaning at the way she tightened around him intimately, as if she couldn't get enough of him, as if she were stroking and holding him in the most sensual, intimate way possible.

The combination of her rocking movements and her little, breathless gasps undid him. He felt the force of his peak vibrate from head to toe. Feeling aftershocks rocking through both him and Callie, he rolled to his side and held her tightly against him.

Her breath tickled his throat and he felt an odd warmth unfurl from inside him. He couldn't remember feeling so satisfied, so complete.

Callie wiggled slightly and slid her arms underneath his. "I know guys like you probably hate this, but could you hold me a little longer?"

Brock frowned. "What do you mean *guys like me?*"

"Well, I mean experienced guys, love-'em-and-leave-'em types. You probably would prefer me to jump up, give you a quick kiss good-night then leave you in peace, but—"

Brock swore and shook his head. "You must have one helluva low opinion of me."

Callie looked up at him. "Not at all. I just understand that you don't want a cling-wrap kind of lover."

Brock felt the stab of truth in her words. She wasn't that far off. With just about any other woman, right now he'd be thinking about how to get her out the door. But not with Callie. He liked the way she felt wrapped around him like cling wrap. He liked feeling every inch of her and he wasn't inclined to move one millimeter away.

"There's no rush," he said, and liked the way her eyes softened.

"Are you sure?" she asked in a husky voice that felt warm and fuzzy inside him.

"Yeah," he said and pulled her against him. She gave a soft sigh of contentment that seeped through him like brandy. He wanted another shot.

They made love frequently over the next few days. Callie seemed determined to make love with Brock in every way she'd been denied in the past, and Brock was perfectly willing to indulge her every request. For a woman who claimed limited experience and previous sexual shyness, she sure was knocking his socks off on a regular basis.

It would have been one hundred percent pleasurable if he hadn't detected an undertone of desperation. He wanted to ask her about it, but some form of self-preservation told him not to go there.

One night after she'd burned up his bed, she sat up and wrapped her arms around her legs. "I have to go to my mother-in-law's house tomorrow morning."

Her announcement felt as if she'd thrown a bucket of ice water on him. He sat up slowly. "Why is that?"

"The memorial for Rob is this weekend. I promised I would come."

He nodded, feeling a tightness form in his chest. He'd spent a lot of time running from thoughts of Rob and how he would feel about Brock making love to his wife. If he spent more than ten seconds thinking about it, Brock felt like the very devil himself. "Do you want me to go with you?"

"No," she said immediately, and he felt the cut as if she'd sliced him with a switchblade. "I think it would be hard for his mother to see you. She's still so hurt. She doesn't understand why—"

"Why I lived and he didn't," he finished for her, bitterness backing up in his throat.

She swallowed audibly, clearly dealing with her own emotions. "I was going to say that she doesn't understand why he had to die. I know that his death and your life aren't really related, but she might react to you out of her pain. Nobody needs that to happen."

"If I had never met Rob, would you want me to go with you?"

She bit her lip and shook her head.

Something inside him cracked and it hurt like hell.

"I have a role to play for my mother-in-law and for the community."

"Grieving widow."

"Right," she said. She reached out and took his hand. "I'm not exactly the grieving widow when I'm with you."

"You have been," he said, soothed just a little by her stroking fingers.

"Not lately."

"You sound like you feel guilty."

"I do, some. If I think about it, but I try not to."

She took a deep breath and exhaled. "I feel very alive with you."

"That's not all bad, Callie," he said, leaning toward her and nuzzling her head.

"I guess," she said, and was quiet for a long moment. "When do you start your job in Atlanta?"

"Nine days."

She gave a forced laugh and pulled away. "Well, at least you won't have to put up with my craziness anymore."

He hated her withdrawal. He wanted her back, close to him, depending on him. "You haven't heard me complaining, have you?"

"No."

"It doesn't have to end when I move to Atlanta," he ventured, tugging at her hand.

"Yes, it does," she said firmly. "You and I have given ourselves permission to be lovers for a limited time. You need to start your life and I need to get on with mine. We both knew this was going to be tempor—"

He covered her mouth with his, cutting off her words with a kiss. His heart pounded in rebellion at the thought of being temporary to her. For the first time in his life, Brock didn't want to be temporary and he didn't know what to do about it.

The following morning, despite Callie's protests, Brock checked the oil and fluids in her little Nissan. He filled up the gas tank and added some air to one of the tires. "Take care of yourself," he said, and watched her drive away. She was going to North Carolina. He would drive to Atlanta in preparation for another change. It was almost time to move on. His job with Callie was nearly done.

Twelve

Marine Lingo Translation
Crucible: A grueling 54-hour training exercise for recruits during boot camp characterized by lack of sleep, little food, forced exercise and teamwork.

Within twelve hours, Brock drove to Atlanta, turned in his rental car, bought an SUV and signed a three-month lease for a furnished executive condo. He wanted to live somewhere temporary and convenient, so he could take his time figuring out where he eventually wanted to settle. Everything he did, everything decision he made, he wondered what Callie would choose.

She would probably turn her nose up at the SUV, preferring something smaller and more fuel efficient, but she might approve of the executive condo. She would change the furnishings, but she would like the skylights and generous expanse of windows.

She would, however, hate the traffic and the busy pace. She would miss the ocean.

He would miss it, too, he thought, as he returned to South Carolina. But he would miss Callie a whole lot more.

As he returned to the small coastal town, Brock gave himself a harsh lecture, reminding himself of the mission he'd intended to complete with Callie. He had accomplished his goal of prying her out of her hermitlike existence. She was able to work now. When he left, she would go out with people. She'd already met the kindergarten teacher for lunch once. He was confident she wouldn't hide away in her little cottage like she had before. He wondered when she would start dating again, and the prospect bothered him so much he turned the radio on full blast to drown out his thoughts.

Instinctively drawn to her place instead of his, Brock pulled into her driveway and noticed that her car wasn't there. She hadn't returned. He wondered how the weekend had gone for her. It was silly as hell, but he wished she had let him join her. More than that, it had stung when she'd told him not to come.

Noticing he was tapping his foot against the floor and drumming his thumb on the steering wheel, he shook his head at his restlessness and got out of the car. He walked toward the beach. It was dark outside, but the smell of salt filled his nostrils and the breeze moved over him with a cleansing rush.

The wind, however, couldn't wash thoughts of Callie from his mind. He hadn't realized how deeply she'd burrowed her way under his skin. Before he'd met her face-to-face, he'd been drawn to her. He'd envied Rob, then when Rob had died, he'd been tormented by visions of her. When he'd become her lover, he'd thought she would quickly lose appeal. He kept waiting, but it wasn't happening.

His gut tightened at the realization. The reflection of a headlight flashed to his left and he turned, spotting a car pulling into her driveway. His heart picked up. She was back.

Brock walked to the house just as she got out of her car and stretched. "Long drive?"

She stopped midstretch and looked at him. "Oh, I thought it might be you. New wheels?" she asked, tilting her head in the direction of his SUV.

He nodded as he moved toward her. "Yeah. I decided it was time to ditch the rental and make a commitment."

"Definitely a guy car," she said.

He'd predicted this. His lips twitched. "You don't like it. Too big, and bad gas mileage."

"Exactly," she said. "And I would have preferred you choose a different color than black."

"Why? Not artsy enough?" he asked, inhaling her scent and wanting to get closer so he could smell her more.

She shook her head. "Safety reasons, knuckle-head," she said, gently stabbing her finger against his chest. "Black is one of the least visible colors for cars. There's a time for stealth and a time to be seen."

His heart twisting, he grabbed her hand and held it against his chest. "Aw, Callie, I didn't know you cared," he said, making sure he used a playful tone.

She rolled her eyes. "Don't get excited. I care for my cat, too."

"Thanks," he said dryly. "I'll remember that."

He looked at her for a long moment that stretched into two and told his stomach to unknot itself. "You okay?" he asked in a low voice.

She sighed and her eyelids fluttered down, shielding her gaze from his. "Yeah." She swallowed. "It hurt, but I didn't feel so lost." She shrugged and looked up at him. "It's hard to explain."

"You don't have to if you don't want," he said, lifting his hand to touch her hair.

"Let's go inside. I've been sitting in that car a long time and I need to tinkle."

Brock chuckled. "You go on in and I'll unload your car."

"Don't forget the wine. I picked up some on my way into town," she said as she dashed for the front door.

"You did?" he muttered in surprise, not sure what to make of that. Not sure he should make anything of it. Maybe she'd planned to drink a glass of wine in solitude after her long drive. Maybe the wine purchase had nothing to do with him.

Brock swore under his breath. He was overthinking stuff way too much. Grabbing her overnight bag, a backpack and the small grocery bag, he took them into her cottage. He set her overnight bag and backpack in her bedroom then took the grocery bag into the kitchen. He stuck the wine in the freezer, setting his mental timer for twenty minutes. He was about to throw away the grocery bag when he spotted four chocolate chip cookies from the deli.

"I had a burger on the way home, but I thought cookies and wine sounded good," she said from the doorway. "Two for you and two for me."

He chuckled. So she had thought of him after all. "You could save the other two for tomorrow night."

"I can share," she said, almost flirting with him. "Tell me about your trip."

He shrugged. "Not much to tell. I bought the SUV and rented a furnished condo."

"Furnished," she echoed, wrinkling her nose in disapproval.

"It's temporary," he said. "It's pretty nice. Got skylights and a Jacuzzi."

"Ooh, I could be a little jealous of the Jacuzzi, but I'll console myself with my ocean and lack of traffic."

"Your ocean," he returned, laughing. "When did it become yours?"

"Okay, my access to the ocean." She crossed her arms over her chest. "I know I've been a pain in the butt fix-it project for you, but you'll miss me more than you plan on."

He sure as hell hoped not, Brock thought. He'd missed her so much this past weekend it had taken his breath away a few times. "Sure I'll miss you. Like a toothache," he teased her as he pulled her against him. He was tired of waiting to hold her.

She thumped his chest with her fist. "It's gonna be weird not having you around."

"I'm only a phone call away. Just a four-hour drive."

She bit her lip and shook her head. "I'm not going to bug you when you're starting your new adventure."

"What if I don't think of it as bugging me?"

She shook her head again. "That's just your over-developed sense of responsibility talking."

He wanted to argue, but shelved it for another time. Now, at least, she was in his arms. "I'm not feeling responsible right now," he said and lowered his head.

"Oh, really? Wha—"

He took her mouth with his, stopping her words. She immediately lifted her hands to the back of his neck and his heart turned over. He took his time with her mouth, kissing her so long he had to pull back for air.

"You feel so good," she whispered. "The whole drive home, I thought about how good you feel."

The sensual need in her voice pulled every chain inside him. "I thought about you a lot, too," he muttered.

"You don't sound happy about it," she murmured, running her lips over his throat.

Brock wasn't happy about it. He felt his body temperature rise another degree. Impatient with her clothes, with his clothes, with anything between them, he slid his fingers over her nipples and approved the ripple that raced through her.

He felt her tug his shirt loose and slip her hands underneath. He felt so hot he wondered if his skin sizzled at her touch. A groan escaped his throat when she pulled at the buttons on his shirt.

"I was planning on wine, cookies then you, but…" Her voice trailed off as she pressed her open mouth on his chest.

Brock groaned again. "We can have the wine. It just needs to chill a little longer."

"That'll take too long," she protested, lowering her mouth to his belly.

Brock swore. "No, it won't. I put it in the freezer."

She glanced up at him. "How long?"

"Fifteen or twenty minutes," he said, his heart pounding at the dark, wanting expression in her eyes.

She bit her lip and lowered her palm to the front of his pants. "I think you're ready now."

Unbearably aroused by her boldness, he held his breath. "Seems like I'm always ready around you."

She closed her eyes and pressed her mouth against his chest. "But I'm ready, too. I've been ready for you for hours."

Brock started to sweat. "You're making it impossible for me to go slow with you."

"I don't want slow tonight," she said, pulling her shirt over her head and tossing her bra aside. "I just want you."

Something inside him snapped. He felt hard and

urgent, almost desperate. No almost about it. He felt lust and something more. He wanted to give and take, to possess. He couldn't rebel against the primitive need. He wanted Callie to be his and no one else's. He wanted to mark her as his. Feeling his muscles twitch from the strain of restraint, he argued with himself. Until she took his mouth. And then he was lost to everything but her.

Sliding his hands under her bottom, he picked her up and strode to her bedroom. It was dark except for the light streaming in from the hallway. He tumbled her onto the bed and immediately followed her down. His mouth seeking hers, he helped rid her of her clothes and his. Her skin felt like the softest satin beneath him—hot satin. He touched her between her thighs and found her damp and ready.

"Do I need a con—"

She shook her head. "I took care of—"

Unable to wait one more second, he thrust inside her. Her sigh mingled with his.

"Take me," she pleaded. "Let me take you."

She already had taken him, he thought, as he began to move inside her in a rhythm guaranteed to send him over the edge in no time. He held her as she urged him on and from the corner of his eye, he saw her bedside table with Rob's photo, his medals and his cover… Even as Brock tumbled over the edge, something inside him whispered *you'll never really have her.*

That didn't keep him from trying. Remembering

the bottle of wine in the freezer, he collected it along with some glasses and toasted every inch of her starting with her hair. He toasted her eyes and nose, which made her giggle. He toasted her lips several times, then her chin. He spilled a little wine on her and kissed it away. She returned the favor, and pretty soon he ditched the wine. She tasted better anyway.

He made love to her again and again throughout the night, trying to get enough of her, trying to fill himself up enough that maybe he wouldn't want her so much.

When dawn slipped through her bedroom window he was sexually satisfied, sated. Sighing, he looked at her, but she was turned away from him. He felt an odd gnawing sensation in his gut. He wanted to see her face. Her hair spilled over the pillow behind her and she was very still. Sleeping, he thought, until he saw her chest rise in a jerky movement and heard a tight choking sound.

Alarmed, Brock sat up. "Callie?" He glanced in the same direction she was looking and his heart sank. She was looking at Rob's medals and his cover, his photo. He heard her sniff and his stomach twisted. "Callie," he said, reaching for her.

She flinched away from his touch.

That slight movement sliced him.

Pulling the sheet with her, she sat up, swiping at her cheeks. "I'm sorry. It just hit me all of a sudden." Her voice was strained and tight. "I kept it together all weekend. I got a little sad at the memorial when

I thought about Rob and me and some of the things we did when we were kids, but—" She broke off and closed her eyes, taking a steadying breath. She opened her eyes and met his gaze. "I'm really starting to lose him," she whispered, desperation oozing from her. "I don't think about him every other minute anymore."

He took her hand in his even though it hurt not to pull her into his arms. "You're not losing him, Callie. You're just starting to live again. He'll always be a part of you, your art, the way you look at people. He'll always be with you even when you're not thinking about him."

There was so much more he wanted to say, more he wanted to be to her. Rob may have been Callie's history, but Brock wanted to be her future. The desire was starting to consume him. He was beginning to think that going through the grueling Crucible training in boot camp had been nothing compared to what he'd gotten himself into with Callie.

He met her for a midmorning walk. It was a windy, sunny day and she chattered excitedly about how much progress she was making with her art. Her voice sounded like music to him. One more thing he would miss like hell. He hated the way his gut felt, like it was being twisted and torn out of him.

She reached for his hand and pulled him to a stop, laughing. "You haven't said a word and you're walking like you're headed for Egypt. What's up?"

He paused, memorizing how her hand felt on his—soft and small, yet firm. "Not Egypt," he said, meeting her gaze. "Just Atlanta."

Her smile fell and she brushed her hair out of her face. "How soon?"

"Today."

Her eyes widened and she looked away. "Wow."

"Callie," he began, wanting to reassure her.

She lifted her hand and shook her head. "No, no, no. You don't have to baby me. I knew this was coming. I'll be okay. I *am* okay," she corrected, lifting her lips in a forced, but determined smile. "You don't have to worry. I won't weep and wail. I won't act like Velcro. I won't be plastic cling wrap around you."

What if that was what he wanted? "You know you can call me for anything," he said. "I can be here in no time if you need me."

"But I won't," she insisted, lifting her chin. "I appreciate everything you've done. You pulled me out of my hole and—" She broke off and shook her head smiling. "God rest Rob's soul, but you gave me the best sex I've ever had."

"Same," he said.

Her eyes widened in surprise. "I find that difficult to believe."

"Believe it," he said.

She met his gaze and the electricity between them hummed as if a power line ran straight through them. Her face turned pink and she lifted her hand self-consciously to her throat. "Watch out," she warned. "It'll go to my head."

"That's fair. You've gone to my head." That was as close as he would get to telling her how he really felt about her. He wouldn't make promises she wouldn't want him to keep. He wouldn't make a profession that would make her faint in disbelief.

She rolled her eyes and snagged his arm. "Come on. I don't want you worrying about me while you go off on your new adventure," she said as she urged him toward her cottage. "I'm going to be fine. I have another luncheon date and I've somehow gotten myself committed to working with kindergartners once a week."

"I guess that means you'll at least start your car once a week."

She tossed him a dirty look then continued with a driven air. "Don't pull that innocent routine with me. I know you're behind it. I'm also going back to the retirement center. But I have something I want you to take with you. There were actually two things I wanted to give you, but I didn't know you were leaving so soon."

Brock shook his head as they entered the back door of the cottage. "I don't want anything, don't need anything. Really. It's not—"

"This isn't anything that big, just a reminder," she said, guiding him to the kitchen. "I'm glad I went ahead and got them developed." She grabbed a packet of photographs from the counter and flipped through them. "Where is it...here it is!" she said, pulling out one and thrusting it at him.

"What was I saying?" she murmured, lifting her hand to her head. "Oh, it's a reminder. Not of me," she said firmly, "but of you."

Distracted by the unusual frantic pace of her conversation, Brock looked down at the photograph and wrinkled his brow in confusion. It was the photo of him and Callie and all those kids who had worked on the sand castle. His gaze automatically returned to Callie, with her sunburned nose, windblown hair and laughing smile.

"Are you looking at yourself?"

He nodded, lying, his gaze still fastened on her.

"See how relaxed you look, how happy," she said, pointing at him.

Brock glanced at himself in the photo. She was right. He looked happy. "Yeah," he muttered.

"Don't forget the sand castles," she said.

He looked at her. "What do you mean?"

"I mean you are one of the most driven men I've ever met. You're intense, sometimes too serious, and almost always too hard on yourself. Don't forget what your dreams were when you were a kid." She took a quick breath then lifted her lips to his in a kiss that didn't last nearly long enough. "Draw some high-rise sand castles during some of those endless meetings."

A terrible knot formed in his throat, but he smiled over it. "I'll do that," he said, and lifted his hand to touch her cheek, memorizing her features one more time. "Call me for any reason."

She shook her head. "This is your new adventure. I refuse to butt in." She bit her lip. "Thank you for everything. Good—"

Unable to bear hearing those words from her, he covered her mouth. "Don't say it."

"What do you want me to say?" she asked, her voice reflecting a hint of the desperation he felt.

"See you soon," he said.

"What if that's not true?"

"Say it anyway."

"See you soon," she said, and he pulled her into his arms and held her in silence for two and a half minutes. It took him that long to get himself squared away enough to walk away.

Thirteen

Marine Lingo Translation
Semper Fi: Marine Corps motto—
Always Faithful.

The late November rain pounded against the window of Brock's corner office. His leg always ached when there was a cold rain and today was no different. Reports waited for his review, but he picked up the photograph of Callie and him with the super sand castle instead. He'd touched it so often, the edges had started to show some wear, so he'd put it in a Plexiglas frame. If he closed his eyes, he could smell the ocean and hear her laughter.

"Brock?" a male voice called from the doorway, interrupting Brock's trip to the South Carolina shore.

Sighing, he turned toward the door. He knew the

voice belonged to the managing partner's intern. "What do you need, Eugene?"

"Mr. Robertson just wants your opinion on this as soon as you can take a look at it," Eugene said, setting down a thick file and glancing over Brock's shoulder. "Pretty lady," he said. "I didn't know you were married."

Brock set the picture down. "I'm not."

"Significant other? Fiancée?" Eugene paused. "Sister? She doesn't really look—"

"No, she's not my sister," he said, feeling irritated. "She's just a woman I know."

"An acquaintance," Eugene clarified, nodding his head.

"Yes," Brock said, knowing the description wasn't right. "And—"

"More," Eugene said, waving his hand. "A friend."

"Why are we playing charades?" Brock asked.

Eugene shrugged. "I've never noticed that photograph before."

That was because Brock had kept it in his drawer until he'd put it in a frame. "You can tell Mr. Robertson I'll get this done by tomorrow."

Eugene scratched the back of his neck. "If you're not romantically involved, I know a woman who would like to meet you for a drink."

Brock immediately rejected the idea. He wasn't interested. He wasn't sure when he would be interested again. He was starting to wonder if he might as well become a monk. "I've got a lot of work—"

"Before you say no," Eugene said, "remember, it's just a drink. I'll pay."

Brock frowned in confusion. "Why?"

Eugene sighed and looked over his shoulder as if to make sure no one was listening. "Because I want Linda in Accounting to go out with me. She said she would meet me for drinks if I could get you to come along for Beth. We could all go together."

Brock couldn't remember meeting Beth person-ally, but she looked exactly like the kind of woman who would have attracted him before Callie. Killer body, clearly experienced, hot. Not feeling a lick of interest, Brock shook his head. "Sorry, Eugene, you're gonna have to—"

"Oh, come on. It's no skin off your nose. One drink." Eugene pointed to the pile of papers on Brock's desk. "It's not like you'll be doing anything better. It looks like all you do is work."

In other circumstances, Brock would be tempted to deliver a kiwi-injection—otherwise known as a swift kick in the rear—to Eugene, but he couldn't ig-nore the pinch of truth in the graduate student's words. Was he becoming a hermit, buried in his work? Disliking the thought, he frowned. "Okay, to-morrow after work. One drink."

Eugene immediately brightened, swinging his fist through the air. "Great. You won't regret it." He low-ered his voice in a confidential tone. "I hear Beth is downright easy for the right guy. You could get lucky."

Quit while you're ahead, Brock thought, but stifled the words. "One drink tomorrow after work," he repeated. "If you don't mind, close the door on your way out," Brock said, scowling as the young man left.

Scrubbing his hand through his hair, he picked up the photo again and drank in the sight of Callie. His gut twisted with longing. What he wouldn't give just to see her again, but she'd made it clear he was temporary. She didn't want anything permanent with him.

He missed her.

Yes, he could function without her. Yes, he was able to feed himself, get his work done and even watch a ballgame. But nothing was half as much fun.

Heaven help him, he was one sorry sonofabitch. He shoved the photo into a drawer so he wouldn't see it. Maybe he needed to forget her. Maybe he needed to go out with Beth and have a few too many and then maybe have Beth, too.

The following afternoon it rained again. His leg was killing him as he held an umbrella and escorted Beth Pritchard to a trendy bar two blocks away from the office. He and Beth followed Eugene and Linda. She had great legs, a killer body and a voice that made him want to chew glass. He'd only noticed her across the room before, so he hadn't known she possessed such a nasal, grating tone.

She chatted about her family and college background and attempted to engage Brock in conversation. By the time the foursome arrived at the bar, Brock was ready for a double of anything hard to drink.

"Eugene tells me you were a Marine," Beth said, scooting her bar stool close to his. "Did you see any action?"

Brock nodded. "What do you want to drink?"

"A sour apple martini," she said.

"Whiskey," he said to the bartender. "Double."

"Tell me what it was like being a Marine," she said. "I have a thing about men in uniform."

"I don't wear it anymore," he said.

She slid her hand onto his thigh. "That's okay. It's what's underneath that really matters."

Caught off guard at her brazenness, he swiveled toward the bar, away from her touch. "The drinks are here."

"Do you like to dance?"

I did with Callie, he thought, remembering dancing with her and how she had felt like magic in his arms. "I haven't done much dancing since I left the Corps. One of my legs was injured and—"

"Oh, that's too bad," she said. "I bet you could slow dance, though."

With the right woman, he thought. *Aw, hell, this wasn't going well at all.* He downed his whiskey in two gulps. "Listen, I don't really feel like being here tonight, so—"

She leaned closer and slid her hand onto his thigh again. "We can go to my house."

He sighed. "Beth, I'm—"

"Excuse me," a familiar female voice said from a few feet away. "Pardon me. Is Brock Armstrong here?"

Unable to believe his ears, he swiveled around to find Callie standing in front of the bar looking like a drowned rat as she gripped a drooping bouquet of roses in one hand and the heel of her shoe in the other.

"Callie?" was all he could say.

Her gaze swiveled away from the bartender to his and his heart tripped over itself.

"Surprise," she said with an unsteady smile. "It's me. I got a makeover at one of the salons this morning, but the rain washed it away. I broke the heel of my shoe on a manhole." She glanced at Beth. "Am I interrupting?"

"Not at all," he said.

Beth frowned. "I'm Beth Pritchard. Brock and I work together."

Callie nodded. "How nice for you. I'm Callie Newton. Brock and I got to know each other this summer." He saw the moment she noticed Beth's hand on his thigh. She bit her lip, looking suddenly uncertain. "You know, maybe this is a bad time. Maybe this was a bad idea."

Feeling a slice of desperation cut through him, he stood and reached for her arm. "No, it was a great idea. I've picked up the phone to call you too many times to count."

She glanced at Beth again. "Uh-huh," she said,

clearly unconvinced. She squeezed her forehead. "I think I've been way too impulsive and—"

"Callie," he interrupted, putting his hands on both her shoulders and gently shaking. "Why are you here?"

She met his gaze and opened her mouth, then closed it. Her gaze slid to Beth and back to Brock. "Are you and her—" She broke off and shook her head. "Oh, I shouldn't ask. I have no right to ask. It's none of my business and—"

"We're not," Brock said. "We're not anything. This is the first time I've been out since I moved to Atlanta. Eugene twisted my arm because he wanted to get with Linda. This was part of the trade-off."

Brock held his breath while Callie paused and studied him. "So you're not involved," she said.

"Not at all," he said. "Why are you here, Callie?" he asked, unable to take his gaze off of her.

She took a careful breath and lifted her chin as if she were fortifying herself. "I want to ask you a favor," she said.

"A favor?" he echoed, confused as hell.

"Well I wasn't going to say favor," she amended and swore under her breath. "I had this all planned out and practiced it on the drive down and I can't remember a freakin' word of it now. Here," she said, thrusting the roses into his arms. "These are for you."

Touched and surprised, he gaped at her. "For me?"

"Yes, and this, too," she said, pulling a CD from the purse hanging on her shoulder.

"Whoa. What's—" He glanced at the CD. "Jimmy Buffet?"

"I'm here to kidnap you. I'm going to the Caribbean and I would like to take someone very special with me." She bit her lip. "That someone very special would be you."

Too shocked for words, all he could do was stare at her, his heart pounding so hard he could hear it throb in his brain.

She pulled back slightly, color rising to her cheeks. "See? I told you it was impulsive, insane, crazy. I shouldn't have—"

"When does the plane leave?" he asked, finally finding his voice.

She blinked. "Tomorrow."

"You want to go back to my place and help me pack?"

Her turn to be speechless. She opened her mouth and her jaw worked, but no sound came out. "Are you sure?"

He lifted his hand to cup her jaw. Her skin was so soft, her heart so sweet and his chest squeezed so tight it hurt. This was his chance with her and he was going to take it. He hoped Rob wouldn't mind. "I'm sure," he said.

Twenty-four hours later, they were sharing a chaise lounge watching the sun set. He was drinking a beer. She was drinking a Hurricane.

Sitting between his legs with her hair against his chest, she gave a long sigh. "I'm glad I did this."

"Me, too," he said, burying his face in her hair and inhaling her scent. They'd made love three times, but hadn't talked about anything important.

"I was scared you would say no."

"What gave you the *cojones* to do it then?"

She turned slightly and looked at him. "Well, you did tell me to call you for any reason."

"Yeah," he said with a nod, wanting more from her, but not wanting to ask.

"Regrets?" she asked, searching his face.

"I regret that we've been apart for the last three months," he said quietly, finding it more and more difficult to cover how deep his feelings were for her.

Setting her drink down on the balcony floor beside her, she turned the rest of the way around onto his lap so that she was facing him. "I do and I don't," she said.

He frowned in confusion.

She lifted her hands to his shoulders and traced them with her fingertips. "I know it sounds strange, but I was such a mess when I first met you. You helped pull me out of my black hole and I think I needed to be by myself for a little bit."

His gut tightened. "And now?"

"I want to be strong enough for you," she said, meeting his gaze.

"What?"

"I don't want to always be leaning on you. I don't want you to always lead with me always following." She bit her lip. "I've done that before."

Her eyes were dark with an emotion he sensed was almost as deep as his, but he was almost afraid to hope. "So what do you want, Callie?"

"I want to take turns." She searched for his hand and laced her fingers through his. "What do you want?"

"I don't want to be temporary," he said, hearing the huskiness in his voice, but unable to do a damn thing about it.

"Oh."

Brock put it all on the line. "I'm in love with you," he said. "I want to marry you."

Her eyes widened. "Are you sure?"

"Yeah, I am. But I'm not sure how you feel about me, how you feel about Rob."

She took a deep breath. "I'll always love Rob and he'll always be a part of me. I didn't think I could love again, but I was wrong. This may sound strange to you, but I kinda feel like Rob gave me you."

Something eased inside Brock. Maybe Rob wouldn't hate him for loving Callie.

He lifted her hand to his lips. "When you're near me, it's like the sun is shining even if it's pouring down rain."

"Really?" she asked, her smile lighting her face.

"Yeah, really."

She threw her arms around his shoulders and hugged him. "You're so strong. I had to make sure I was strong enough for you."

"There's brute strength and there's magic. You're the magic."

* * *

Twelve months later, Brock kidnapped his wife and took her on a trip to the Caribbean. She was sipping lemonade and he was drinking a beer. It was afternoon, and she lay between his legs on a chaise lounge with her gorgeous seven-months-pregnant belly exposed to the waning afternoon sun.

She touched her belly and gave a breathless chuckle. Brock had watched her often enough to know what that meant—the baby had moved.

He slid his hand over her stomach and felt a kick. He smiled and stroked her hair with his other hand. "How does cupcake like the Caribbean?" he asked. *Cupcake* was Callie's name for the baby.

She turned slightly and looked up at him with loving eyes that still made his heart turn over. "Cupcake loves the Caribbean. Cupcake is going to be a weekend beach baby."

"Just like Momma," he said. "Have you hated the city as much as you thought you would?" He'd worried about that. She'd been so emphatic about detesting the traffic and noise.

She shook her head. "How could I hate it when I'm with you? Besides, you lured me with such a nice house in a nice woodsy neighborhood and tucked me into a cul de sac. You come home every day and love me every night, and sometimes you even cook dinner. You made peace with my cat and let him move in with us, too."

He lowered his head to taste her lips. Heaven help him, he still couldn't get enough of her.

She sighed in pleasure against his mouth. "Plus you let me kidnap you to the beach almost every weekend." She paused a half beat. "My only complaint is that you won't let me include my drawings of you in my show next month."

Brock chuckled. He knew she was teasing. "I thought your nude drawings of me were supposed to be just for us."

"The artist in me wants to share them. After all, they took so long for me to complete because you kept interrupting me while I was drawing."

He skimmed his hand down her throat to her now-blooming cleavage. "I don't recall you complaining too much at the time."

"Well, you didn't—"

He slid his finger underneath her halter top to touch her nipple. Her breasts had become delightfully sensitive to his touch due to her advancing pregnancy.

She closed her eyes and made a soft breathy sound.

He toyed with both stiff peaks, enjoying her sensual movements.

She opened her eyes. "You're distracting me again."

"It's one of my favorite things to do."

Sighing, she shifted slightly and lifted her lips to kiss him. "I am totally crazy for you, Brock Armstrong."

His heart melted in his chest the same way it did every time she assured him how much she loved him. Sometimes he still couldn't believe she was his.

"I love how you encourage me with my art. I love

how you take care of me and let me take care of you. I love how you helped me make the memory box for Rob and hung it on the wall in the den."

"He's a part of you. I'll always be grateful to him, Callie. I'm sorry we lost him, but he gave me something more precious than I could have dreamed."

Her eyes filled with tears. "I can't believe how lucky I am to have you."

"Same for me, sunshine. I guess we'll just have to keep showing each other." He dropped a kiss on her soft, sweet mouth. Showing her how much he loved her would be his favorite mission for the rest of his life.

* * * * *

DYNASTIES: THE DANFORTHS

A family of prominence...
tested by scandal, sustained by passion.

THE ENEMY'S DAUGHTER
by Anne Marie Winston
(Silhouette Desire #1603)

Selene Van Gelder and Adam Danforth could not
resist their deep attraction, despite the fact that their
fathers were enemies. When their covert affair was
leaked to the press, they each had to face the truth
about their feelings. Would the feud between their
families keep them apart—or was their love strong
enough to overcome anything?

Available September 2004 at your favorite retail outlet.

If you enjoyed what you just read,
then we've got an offer you can't resist!

Take 2 bestselling love stories FREE!

Plus get a FREE surprise gift!

COMING NEXT MONTH

SDCNM0804